This book introduces to th[...]
ing world a grea[...]
today's foremo[...]
ner of the high[...]

HERE IS WHA[...]CAN CRIT-
ICS HAVE ALR[...]DY SAID ABOUT
IT—

"A superb novel in which the problems
arising from a loveless marriage and from
conflicting pulls of old and new ways of
thought and conduct are subtly and mov-
ingly combined."
—N. Y. *Herald Tribune*

"Unusual ability to create beautiful images and to give pleasure."
—*New Yorker*

"An important work both as a revealing
glimpse into the inner spiritual problem
of modern Japan and as a novel of broader
human significance."
—N. Y. *Herald Tribune*

"Engagingly written, often very witty.
There is not a false note in the translation."
—Donald Keene, N. Y. *Times*

Every worm to his taste;
some prefer to eat nettles.

*Japanese proverb*

---

*NOTE*
*on the Pronunciation of Japanese Names*

Consonants are pronounced approximately as in English, except that "g" is always hard, as in Gilbert. Vowels are pronounced as in Italian, and always sounded separately, never as diphthongs. Also as in Italian, the final "e" is always sounded. Thus the name Kaname is pronounced Kah-nah-meh. There is no heavy penultimate accent as in English; it is adequate to accent each syllable equally.

# SOME
# PREFER
# NETTLES

## Junichiro
## Tanizaki

*Translated by*
*Edward G. Seidensticker*

A BERKLEY MEDALLION BOOK
published by
THE BERKLEY PUBLISHING CORPORATION

COPYRIGHT © 1955, BY ALFRED A. KNOPF, INC.

First published in Japan as TADE KUU MUSHI.

Published by arrangement with
Alfred A. Knopf, Inc.

BERKLEY EDITION, NOVEMBER, 1960

BERKLEY MEDALLION BOOKS are published by
The Berkley Publishing Corporation
101 Fifth Avenue, New York 3, New York

Printed in the United States of America

ON SEPTEMBER 1, 1923, the day the earthquake destroyed Tokyo and Yokohama, Tanizaki Junichirō was in the Hakone Mountains south of Yokohama. Almost before he thought to worry about his family in Yokohama, he wrote later, he felt a perverse surge of happiness at the news of the disaster. " 'Now they will make Tokyo a decent city.' I could not keep back the glad thought." The darkness of the old city was gone, and the new city would be filled with horns and headlights, movie theaters, the bright cries of streetwalkers, the radiance of beauty parlors and Turkish baths.

When Tanizaki wrote down these recollections some ten years later, he meant them to tell the story of his early career. He was thirty-seven years old in 1923, and he had been a well-known writer already for more than ten years. He was born of the old Tokyo merchant class, the class that was in charge of Japanese culture when Commodore Perry arrived to open the country, and the class that in 1923 still considered itself rather the finest fruit of the Japanese race; but he disliked both his class and the tradition it stood for. His early works, generally called "demoniac" by the Japanese, were written under the influence less of Japanese predecessors than of Poe, Baudelaire, and Wilde; and in his personal life he seems to have indulged, as the old man of this novel once did, "in foreign tastes of the most hairraising variety." At the time of the earthquake, he was living on the Yokohama "bluff," the very heart of the foreign conclave. Few Japanese went to such extremes even in an age that was fascinated with the West.

After the earthquake he moved to Okamoto, between Kobe and Osaka. Like all natives of Tokyo, he had always viewed Osaka with a mixture of amusement and contempt. The Osakan was a penny-grabbing bumpkin who had not learned the fine Japanese art of concealing his emotions; and the Osakan seemed insensitive to the exhilarating succession of foreign influences that was sweeping the country. He was cloddishly behind the times.

But presently a suggestion that the case was not so clear began to come into Tanizaki's writings. His first major post-earthquake novel, *A Fool's Love,* is a disquieting study of what can happen when one cuts oneself off from one's past. The hero, a young man who will live in the new way, finds a little bar girl who reminds him of Mary Pickford, and he proceeds to groom her so that he need not be ashamed of her in front of the golden-haired foreigners. At the end he is living a comfortless life in Yokohama while his fashionable wife takes foreign lovers.

In 1928 Tanizaki began serial publication of two novels that in effect sum up his early career and announce a new beginning. *Whirlpool* brings up for final review all the perversions and cruelties of the early novels, and leaves its heroine, who has hoped to renounce convention and find sexual liberation thereby, in the darkest despair. *Some Prefer Nettles* is in many ways Tanizaki's own story of a sexually disturbed Tokyo man with rather superficial Western tastes who almost against his will finds himself attracted to Osaka and to the Japanese past. The issue is clearly drawn, these two novels seem to tell us: to be foreign is to court unhappiness; a Japanese can find peace only by being as intensely Japanese as the times will allow.

Between 1931 and 1935 Tanizaki turned out a series of short historical novels, all of them dreamy anthems to a day when beauty did not seem compelled to fight against its time. He was occupied until the war on a rendition into modern Japanese of *The Tale of Genji,* the great eleventh-century Japanese romance. Since the war he has published a massive novel called *Sasame Yuki,* a loving and detailed re-creation of the old Osaka way of life in what even Tanizaki had to admit were its last precarious days. Now he is back at the *Genji,* which he hopes to finish reworking this year.

II

*Some Prefer Nettles* is a personal confession and the story of a cultural conflict. The central situation, an

unhappy marriage between two people who do not interest each other sexually and who feel a tormenting uncertainty over what to do about it, seems to be autobiographical. In August 1930 Tanizaki divorced his wife,
who by previous arrangement became the wife of the poet
and novelist Satō Haruo. Satō has written that one
night after dinner Tanizaki remarked: "How would you
like to marry O-chiyo?" and everything proceeded ami-
cably from there. Tanizaki's first marriage, one judges
from an interview Tanizaki gave the papers at the time
and from Satō's recollections, was not unlike Kaname's
in this novel: Tanizaki had nothing against his wife; she
simply did not interest him. His unhappiness, it appears,
had been growing for some time, and it is clear enough
that he was thinking of his own marriage when he published *Some Prefer Nettles* two years before the divorce.

The novel is also autobiographical, of course, in that
it tells of Tanizaki's growing attachment to Osaka and
traditional Japan. But so much contemporary Japanese
fiction is thinly disguised autobiography that one
pounces with joy on a novel that is more. Tanizaki's career, with its early liking for the West and its subse-
quent retreat into the Japanese past, tells so much
about modern Japan that when he talks about himself he
talks about much more than himself.

The real theme of *Some Prefer Nettles* is the clash
between the new and the old, the imported and the domestic. The marital conflict and the cultural conflict are
in a very general way coextensive. Misako, the wife, is
drawn toward the new and foreign, and Kaname more
and more strongly toward the traditional. And yet each
is pulled by conflicting forces. Misako is the stylish young
matron of the future, but we know that she is by no
means sure of herself, and at the end of the book her
father remarks sagely that her modernness is "a pretty
thin veneer." Kaname for his part longs to bury his
emotional troubles in the calm unity of the old Japanese
way of life, and yet he is attracted to the Eurasian prostitute Louise. If the divorce is to come, one feels, it will
settle more for Kaname than it will for Misako, and
even Kaname has crises ahead.

The new and the old. For Kaname and for Tanizaki

7

there is on the one hand Tokyo and on the other Osaka, and on the one hand the robust Eurasian Louise and on the other the fragile, vaguely unhealthy Japanese doll, O-hisa. Tokyo is the city of foreign fads and of journalism, and of an "intelligentsia" created by the two. "One cannot lightly dismiss the fact," Tanizaki lamented when he published his views of the two cities in 1934, "that Tokyo is the capital of the nation, and Tokyo shallowness is having its effect on every one of our arts."

Osaka, on the other hand, is "the merchants' capital." The Osaka merchant is grasping, says the Tokyo man. "And indeed is it not natural that he should be?" Tanizaki replies. "He may distress you at first, if you are used to Tokyo, but presently you see that his very covetousness is in its way endearing. To me he is more progressive, more virile, he has more substance, than your callow Tokyo intellectual."

The Osaka merchant, quite simply, is still the Osaka merchant, while the Tokyo intellectual is a pale chaser after fads he can make nothing of; and since the culture of old Japan was a merchants' culture, something of it must still remain in Osaka. Even in Osaka it is dying perhaps—the old puppet theater to which Tanizaki gives such affectionate attention in this novel can no longer attract crowds; the motion-picture company that supports it is getting restive. But in Osaka it should still be possible for a little while to live a life that is sufficient to itself.

A tentative acceptance of the merchants' culture sets off the return to old Japan in *Some Prefer Nettles*. The return is in a sense a return to childhood. Kaname, we are told in Chapter Three, "had grown up in the merchants' section of Tokyo before the earthquake destroyed it, and the thought of it could fill him with the keenest nostalgia; but the very fact that he was a child of the merchants' quarter made him especially sensitive to its inadequacies." The urge to go back thus becomes a reaffirmation of a childhood that the adult intellect, if not the adult heart, has rejected. The Osaka song, "Snow," the first bit of Osaka art to which Kaname is attracted, brings memories of his early Tokyo years. The Osaka theater reminds him of an afternoon long ago when he was taken to a theater in Tokyo by his mother. In the last chapter O-hisa, the Kyoto beauty, is quite deprived of sex and reduced to a doll, and we are given to understand that Kaname will henceforth be interested in O-hisa-like dolls. He will have no more of adult problems, he will go back and relive his childhood.

If he does go back, however, it cannot be for long, and Tanizaki knows it. The West is here to stay, and presently Tokyo will have everything its way. "I know as well as anyone," Tanizaki said in 1934 in a sad and rather moving essay on the traditional arts called *In Praise of Shadows*, "that I am dreaming, and that, having come this far, we cannot turn back. I know that I am grumbling to myself and demanding the impossible. But there can be no harm, if my grumblings are taken for what they are, in considering how unlucky we have been, what losses we have suffered, in comparison with the Westerner. The Westerner has been able to move forward in ordered steps, while we have met a superior civilization and have had to surrender to it, and we have had to leave a road we have followed for thousands of years."

Today the prospects for the old civilization seem even dimmer than when these words were written. The war seems to have completed the mischief that Tokyo began. All of the small cities to which we are directed in Chapter Ten if we would find a survival from an earlier day have been destroyed. The Osaka of *Sasame Yuki* is gone. Kyoto survived the bombings, and the earthen walls and the dusky old houses Tanizaki so loves are still to be found there; but inside them one is likely to come on young ladies who cut their hair in the manner of Audrey Hepburn, and young gentlemen who want to go off to Paris to study something called *dessin* or to Peking to learn of Paradise. Kyoto has no novelist of note except Tanizaki, and Tanizaki has no disciples. Yet some things do survive—the Osaka puppet theater, for instance, albeit amid voices prophesying the worst, and even the Awaji puppet theater, about which Tanizaki was even more pessimistic when he wrote *Some Prefer Nettles*. And the conflict that is at the heart of the novel continues to trouble the Japanese spirit. Almost everyone seems now to have chosen the new, but not everyone is happy with it.

9

It is easy to argue that Japanese is a hopelessly vague language from which it is impossible to translate, but the argument usually comes down to an unreal notion of what even the best translator can accomplish. No two languages make quite the same distinctions, and every translation is a makeshift insofar as this is true.

It is undeniable, however, that the refusal of the Japanese language to make distinctions often seems scandalous, and the problems one faces in trying to make Japanese literature understandable in translation grow accordingly. Tanizaki takes the position, in an illuminating study of literary style called *A Composition Reader,* that it is the duty of the Japanese writer to know the genius of his language and to accommodate himself to it: if Japanese is vague, its vagueness must be made a virtue of.

Tanizaki puts himself in a line of stylists stemming from *The Tale of Genji,* stylists who aim at a dreamy, floating prose. They are suspicious of too vivid a choice of words, too clear a view, too conspicuous a transition from one figure or idea to another. They prefer their prose to be misty, to suggest more than it says. They are, Tanizaki says, pure Japanese stylists, in opposition to Chinese-influenced writers who aim at conciseness and precision. One is left to conclude that the latter, who rather dominate the field today, are trying to do something that can only result in violence to the basic nature of the Japanese language.

Among the precepts Tanizaki hands down to those who would be writers are these: Do not try to be too clear; leave some gaps in the meaning. "The modern writer seems to me to be too kind to his reader," he says, and again: "We Japanese scorn the bald fact, and we consider it good form to keep a thin sheet of paper between the fact or the object and the words that give expression to it." Once when he was criticized for not exploring the inner life of one of his characters, he retorted: "But why should I discuss his psychology? Can't the reader guess from what I've already told him?"

These ideas are brought up not to show how difficult

Tanizaki is to translate—the Tanizaki sentence, for all its poetic suggestiveness, is as a matter of fact a model of limpid expression—but rather in the hope that they will throw light on what to the Western reader may be a confused and uncertain ending. In the last chapter of *Some Prefer Nettles* we see that Kaname, the hero, is strongly drawn toward O-hisa, the Kyoto beauty who represents old Japan. We have his statement that he has made a decision for himself, and we know fairly well what the decision is: the old man, with his conservative tastes and his immersion in what still lives of the Japanese past, has come to Kaname as a vision of what he himself will one day be. At the very end we have, dim through linen netting, the pale face of an Awaji puppet, symbol of the disembodied Japanese femininity to which Kaname is turning; and we have O-hisa herself, equally dim and fragile, kneeling beside the door.

But we are not told *exactly* what Kaname will do. Will he appear at the City Hall the next day dramatically announcing his break with the West as he turns in his divorce notice? Or will he choose a compromise whereby for the time being he can have both O-hisa and the Eurasian Louise and can perhaps even shelter his wife, Misako? We do not know. It is at this point that Tanizaki chooses to be "unkind." "And why should I tell you?" we can hear him saying. "I have already told you enough about Kaname. I prefer to leave some gaps."

IV

This does not seem the place for a detailed discussion of the puppet theater that stands for Osaka art and the Osaka past in *Some Prefer Nettles*. The reader will perhaps be less puzzled at descriptions of that theater, however, if he imagines puppets much larger than the familiar Punch and Judy, the principal ones manipulated each by three puppeteers in full view of the audience.

*Love Suicide at Amijima,* which is being played in Chapters Two and Three, is by Chikamatsu Monzaemon, the greatest of writers for the puppet stage. It concerns the love of Jihei, a young Osaka paper merchant, for Koharu, a geisha. Jihei's wife, O-san, attempts to sacrifice herself for their happiness, but the pull of duties and counter-duties becomes too much and Jihei and Koharu kill themselves. *Morning-Glory Diary,* which is described in Chapter Eleven, is a melodrama about a beautiful lady, Miyuki, and a samurai, Komazawa, who love and part. Miyuki presently goes blind. The climax of the play is an Evangelinesque scene where Miyuki discovers just too late that she and Komazawa are stopping at the same inn. She follows him to a river fording, but is kept back by a flood after he has crossed. Unfortunately for the effect, however, she regains her eyesight and finds him after all. One may wish that the playwright had followed Tanizaki's advice and stopped a little sooner.

The cuts of Bunraku puppets and puppeteers at the chapter heads are the work of Mr. Takahashi Sachio of Tokyo, a Kabuki actor whose stage name is Nakamura Tokie. They are repeated twice in this order: Koharu, Jihei, and O-san from *Love Suicide at Amijima;* Komazawa and Miyuki from *Morning-Glory Diary;* and Mitsuhide and his mother Satsuki from *Taikōki,* which is mentioned in Chapter Ten.

The Japanese order in personal names, with the surname first, has been preserved in both this introduction and the translation.

I am indebted to the Ford Foundation for the grant that made experimental work on this translation possible. I am also indebted to Mr. Takahashi Osamu, who went over the manuscript and was most patient with my questions.

*October 1954*                                             E. G. S.

## CHAPTER ONE

"You think you might go, then?" Misako asked several times during the morning.

Kaname as usual was evasive, however, and Misako found it impossible to make up her own mind. The morning passed. At about one o'clock she took a bath and dressed, and, ready for either eventuality, sat down inquiringly beside her husband. He said nothing. The morning newspaper was still spread open in front of him.

"Anyway, your bath is ready."

"Oh." Kaname lay sprawled on a couple of cushions, his chin in his hand. He pulled his head a little to the side as he caught a suggestion of Misako's perfume. Careful not to meet her eyes, he glanced at her—more accurately he glanced at her clothes—in an effort to catch some hint of a purpose that might make his decision for him. Unfortunately, he had not been paying much attention to her clothes lately. He knew vaguely that she gave a great deal of attention to them and was always buying something new, but he was never consulted and never knew what she had bought. He could make out nothing more revealing than the figure of an attractive and stylish matron dressed to go out.

"What would you like to do?" he asked.

"It doesn't really matter. If you're going, I'll go too. If not, I can go to Suma."

"You've promised to go to Suma?"

"Not really. Tomorrow would do as well."

Seated stiffly, her eyes fixed firmly on a spot two or three feet over Kaname's head, Misako began buffing her nails.

Today was not the first time they had been faced with this difficulty. Indeed, whenever they had to decide whether or not to go out together, each of them became passive, watchful, hoping to take a position according to the other's manner. It was as if they held a basin of water balanced between them and waited to see in which direction it would spill. Sometimes the day passed without their coming to a decision, sometimes at the last moment they suddenly knew what they would do. Today was a little different, however. Kaname sensed that they would finally go out together. His refusal even so to be a little more positive was not entirely a matter of perverseness or laziness. He thought of their tense trips alone together, no less tense for being, as today, only the one-hour trip to downtown Osaka. He sensed too what Misako wanted to do. She did not have to go to Suma, she said, but there was not much doubt that she would rather go there to see Aso than be bored at the puppet theater with her father. It seemed necessary somehow to bring her feelings out into the open.

Misako's father had called from Kyoto the day before and asked if the two of them would join him at the theater. Misako had been out, and Kaname had been rash enough to say that they "probably could." As a matter of fact he could not very well have refused. "Let me know the next time you come down for the theater," he had remarked once in a somewhat hypocritical attempt to please the old man. "I haven't been in much too long myself." He had evidently been taken at his word. Then too, quite aside from the play, it was not entirely impossible that he and Misako's father might not have another chance to talk at their ease together. The old man, now nearly sixty, was in retirement in Kyoto, where he lived the life of the conservative man of taste. While Kaname's own tastes were rather different and he was often enough annoyed at the old man's displays of connoisseurship, still the latter had played the gallant in his youth, it was said, and there remained something open and easy in his manner that Kaname found very attractive. The thought that soon they might no longer be father-in-law and son-in-law gave him considerable regret—in fact, he sometimes told himself ironically, the regret at divorcing his father-in-law might be somewhat stronger than the regret at divorcing his wife—and, though ordinarily such an idea would not have troubled him, he wanted one last chance to demonstrate his sense of filial duty.

Still, it was a mistake not to have consulted Misako. He was usually very careful to consider her wishes. She had

14

gone out the evening before "to do some shopping in Kobe," and as he talked to the old man the picture had come into Kaname's mind of the two of them, the old man's daughter and Aso, walking along the shore at Suma, arm in arm, and with it the flicker of a conviction that if she was seeing Aso then, she need hardly see him again the following day. But maybe he was being unjust. Misako never hid things from him. She disliked lying and she had no need to lie, and when she said she was going shopping, perhaps she was indeed going shopping. It was not pleasant, though, for Kaname to be told badly of each visit to Aso, she must know, and perhaps he was not being too suspicious when he took her "shopping in Kobe" to mean something else. In any case, she would not accuse him of malice in having accepted the invitation, he felt sure—and then again, even assuming that she had seen Aso the evening before, she might want to see him again. At first her visits had been fairly infrequent, once every week or ten days, but it was not uncommon now for her to see him two and three days running.

When Kaname came back from the bath, ten minutes or so later, she was still polishing mechanically at her fingernails, her eyes still fixed on the wall.

"Do you want to see it?" she asked.

She avoided looking at him, out on the veranda now, a bathrobe hung loosely from his shoulders, parting his hair in a hand mirror. As she spoke she brought the shiny, pointed nails of her left hand up close to her eyes.

"Not especially. I told him I did, though."

"When?"

"When was it, I wonder. . . . He got so excited about his puppets that I finally nodded back to make him happy."

Misako laughed pleasantly, as she would for the merest acquaintance. "You hardly needed to do that. You've never been that friendly with Father, after all."

"In any case, maybe we ought to stop by for a few minutes."

"Where is the Bunraku Puppet Theater?"

"It's not at the Bunraku. The Bunraku burned down. It's at a place downtown called the Benten."

"That means we sit on the floor? I can't stand it, really I can't. My knees will be agony afterwards."

15

"There's no avoiding it. That's the sort of place people like your father go. His tastes have got a little beyond me—and after the way he used to love the movies. I read somewhere the other day that men who are too fond of the ladies when they're young generally turn into antique-collectors when they get old. Tea sets and paintings take the place of sex."

"But Father hasn't exactly given up sex. He has O-hisa."

"She's one of the antiques in his collection, exactly like an old doll."

"If we go we'll have her inflicted on us."

"Then let's have her inflicted for an hour or two. Think of it as filial piety." Kaname began to feel that Misako had some very special reason for not wanting to go.

She went briskly over to the chest, however, and took out a kimono for him, carefully folded in a paper cover. "You're wearing kimono, I suppose."

Kaname was as careful about his clothes as Misako was about hers. A particular kimono required a particular cloak and a particular sash, and each ensemble was planned down even to accessories like the watch and chain, the wallet, the cloak-cord, the cigarette case. Only Misako understood the system well enough to be able to put everything together when he specified the kimono he would wear. Now that she had taken to going out by herself a good deal, she always made sure before she left that his clothes were laid out for him. Indeed, when he thought of it, that was the only function she really discharged as a wife, the only function for which another woman would not do as well. Particularly when, as today, she stood behind him, helping him into his kimono and straightening his collar, he became most keenly aware of what an eccentric thing their marriage was. Who, looking at them now, could know that they were not really husband and wife? Not even the servants, who saw them every day, seemed yet to have suspected it. And indeed weren't they husband and wife? He thought of how she helped him even with his underwear and socks. Marriage was after all not only a matter of the bedroom. He had known women enough in his life who ministered to that particular need. But surely the reality of marriage lay as much in these other small ministrations. Indeed, he could almost feel that through them marriage was revealing itself in its most basic, its most classical form, and he could think of Misako as an entirely satisfactory wife. . . .

Kaname looked down at the back of Misako's neck as he stood tying his sash. She knelt with a black cloak spread on her knee, attaching the cord for him, and the cord pin drew a sharp black line against the white of her hand. Now and then, as she worked the pin into place, the tips of her softly polished nails met with the slightest click. She perhaps knew from experience what sort of emotions the occasion would arouse in him, and, as if to ward off the possibility that she herself might be drawn into the same sentimentality, she went at her duties precisely, impersonally. That in itself, however, made it possible for him to look down on her, a sort of mute regret rising in him, without fear of meeting her eyes. He saw the curve of her back, he saw the soft roundness of her shoulders in the shadow of her kimono, he saw, where her kimono was kicked aside at the skirt, an inch or two of ankle above her sock, white and crisply starched in the Tokyo manner. Her skin, under these stolen glimpses seemed fresher and younger than her almost thirty years, and had it belonged to someone else's wife he could have found it beautiful and exciting. Even now sometimes in the night he felt a certain desire to press close, to caress it as he had in those first nights after they were married. But the sad thing was that, since those early nights, her skin had quite lost its power to excite him. The very youth and freshness might indeed be due to the fact that he had forced on her a sort of widow's existence—the thought came to him less sad than strangely chilling.

"And it's such a beautiful day." She had the cord ready and moved around to help him into the cloak. "It seems a shame to waste it in a theater."

Kaname felt her hand brush against his neck two or three times, but her touch was as cool and impersonal as a barber's.

"Shouldn't you telephone Aso?" He suspected that she was thinking of more than the weather.

"No. . . ."

"I wish you would."

"It isn't at all necessary."

"Won't he be waiting?"

Misako hesitated. "I suppose so. . . . When will we be back?"

"If we go now and stay for an act or so, we should be out by five or six."

"I wonder if it would be too late to go to Suma then."

"It probably wouldn't be too late, but we don't know what plans your father has. If he wants us to go to dinner we can't very well refuse. . . . All in all, maybe you ought to wait till tomorrow."

As he finished speaking, a maid came in to say that Misako had a call from Suma.

## CHAPTER TWO

MISAKO was at the telephone for a half-hour before it was agreed that the next day would do as well. She still looked pensive and unhappy when toward three o'clock they left the house. These expeditions alone together were becoming more and more of a rarity.

They did sometimes go out on Sunday afternoons with Hiroshi, who was in the fourth grade. Hiroshi had in a vague way sensed that something was wrong, and it seemed necessary to reassure him. But how many months had it been since they had gone out quite alone? Kaname was sure that Hiroshi would be much less hurt at having been left out than delighted when he got back from school and found that the two of them had gone off together.

Whether it was good to reassure him Kaname did not really know. The child was over ten, after all, and unless he is feeble-minded a child that age reacts not too differently from an adult. "Isn't he clever?—he seems to have guessed when no one else has," Misako once said. Kaname laughed. "Of course he has. Any child would, and only a mother would be surprised at it." Clearly he would one day have to tell Hiroshi everything, to appeal to his reason. Kaname did not doubt that the boy would understand, and to deceive him seemed as reprehensible as to deceive a grownup. Neither he himself nor Misako was wrong, Kaname would say; what was wrong was outdated convention. The time would come when a child need think nothing of having divorced parents. He would go on being their child, and he could visit one or the other as he chose.

So Kaname would explain it one day. But in the meantime he could not be sure that he and Misako would not have a reconciliation, and in any case it seemed pointless to upset Hiroshi any earlier than was necessary. The "one day" therefore continued to be postponed, and, in the desire to see the boy happy, the two of them occasionally put on bright connubial expressions and went out for a walk with him. But the intuitive powers of a child that age were remarkable, Kaname sometimes thought. Hiroshi was probably quite beyond being deceived, and indeed he was perhaps acting a part as carefully as they were, hiding his troubles from them, trying to make them happy as they were trying to make him happy. The three of them would go out for their walk, each alone with his thoughts, each feigning easy, pleasant family affection. The picture was a little frightening. That his and Misako's conspiracy to deceive the world should have been allowed to include Hiroshi seemed to Kaname rather a serious crime.

He could not bring himself to flaunt his marriage as a model for the new morality, the convention-free future. He had a strong case, he felt, and his conscience was clear against the day when he might have to defend himself; but he hardly liked the thought of going out of his way to put himself in a doubtful position. He preferred to live quietly, unobtrusively, casting no dishonor on his ancestors, a member of the leisure class—a marginal member perhaps, but still a member—with the capital, somewhat diminished, that his father had left, and with at least the nominal title of director of his father's company. He himself had little to fear from meddling relatives, but his wife's position was more dangerous. Unless he protected her he could easily find that they had both become shackled quite beyond hope of winning back any ground for movement. What, for instance, if rumors were to spread abroad and the old man in Kyoto, broad-minded though he might be, were to feel himself compelled for the sake of public opinion to disown her? "That worries me not in the least. I can get along quite well without my family," Misako herself said, but as a practical matter could she? Aso had a family too, and with her reputation ruined she might find that even if she freed herself from Kaname she could not go to him. And what of Hiroshi? What would his future be with a social outcast for a mother? If they were to be happy once they had parted, everything considered, it seemed wise for the moment at least to maintain the pretense of a marriage and to work quietly toward an understanding that would alienate no one. To keep the world from looking in on them, they gradually narrowed their circle of associations. There were still occasions, however, when they had to put on their disguises and act their parts, and Kaname always felt guilty and unhappy when they came up.

Perhaps Misako did too and that was why she had seemed so reluctant to go out with him today. She was in many ways timid and indecisive, but she had a hard core that made her resist the demands of custom, duty, friendship, more strongly than Kaname himself could. She did not seem to mind acting with a certain restraint for the sake of Kaname and Hiroshi, but she did not care to display herself as a wife any more than she had to. It was not only that she disliked the deception. She had Aso to consider. He understood the situation and acquiesced in it, but he expected her to appear in public as little as possible, and he would hardly be pleased if he heard that she and Kaname had for no very good reason gone to the theater together in the heart of the very busiest part of Osaka. Whether Kaname sensed none of this or sensed it all and saw no point in worrying about it she could not say, and it added to her impatience not to be able to tell him clearly what was disturbing her. Surely there was no reason for him to go on cultivating her father. It would have been another matter, of course, if it had seemed that the old man was to go on being "father" to Kaname indefinitely, but with the end of the relationship so near, were there not indeed reasons why it might be better to be more aloof? It would only upset the old man the more to hear of the divorce after this careless display of filial piety.

The two of them, with their separate thoughts, boarded the train for downtown Osaka. The early cherries were just coming into bloom. For all the brilliance of the late-

March sun, there was still a touch of winter in the air. Kaname's sleeve, where the black silk showed under his light spring cloak, glittered in the sun like sand along the seashore. As he pulled his hands inside his kimono he felt a touch of cold air down his back. He disliked the patches of winter underwear one so often sees at the neck and sleeves of a kimono, and even in the coldest weather he wore only a long under-kimono next to his skin.

The car was half empty, it being an off hour, and at each station a few passengers unhurriedly got on and out. The roof was painted a fresh white, sending a strong light into the deepest corners and making the faces of the passengers look somehow bright and healthy. Misako had taken a seat on the side of the car opposite him. She sat with her shawl pulled over the lower part of her face, reading a small volume of translations. The white cloth cover, fresh from the bookstore, was clean and sharp as a sheet of metal, and her fingers against the binding were clothed in sapphire-colored silk net gloves, the pointed fingernails glowing softly through the tiny openings.

Almost always when they went out together they took up their positions thus. If Hiroshi was between them it was a different matter, but if they were alone, side by side, the one feeling the warmth of the other, it seemed more than uncomfortable, it seemed almost immoral. One of them therefore would wait for the other to find a seat, and then carefully take a seat on the other side. To guard against the danger that their eyes might meet, Misako always had something with her to read, and as soon as she sat down she erected a screen in front of her eyes.

At Osaka station Kaname tore a ticket from his book and let Misako take care of her own, and with a precision that suggested careful planning they walked out into the plaza two or three paces apart. Kaname stepped into a taxi first, Misako followed. For the first time they were alone, husband and wife; but had anyone been watching them in their glass box, he would have seen them, like silhouettes pasted on paper, forehead against forehead, nose against nose, jaw against jaw, facing stiffly forward, shaking slightly with the motion of the taxi.

"What is playing?" Misako asked.

"*Love Suicide,* he said, and something else. I've forgotten."

As if forced to one concession by the long silence, each made his one remark. They gazed rigidly forward as they spoke, the one seeing the line of the other's nose dimly through the corner of the eye.

Misako, who had no idea where the Benten Theater was, had no choice but to follow when they left the cab. Kaname had apparently received instructions from the old man. They went first to a teahouse that catered to theater guests, and were guided from there by a kimono-clad maid. Misako felt more and more oppressed as the time approached when she would have to appear before her father and play the part of the wife. She pictured him on his cushion in the pit, his eyes fixed on the stage, a saké cup raised to his lips, and beside him his mistress, O-hisa. Misako felt tense and uncomfortable with her father, but O-hisa she actively disliked. O-hisa, younger than Misako, was a tranquil, unexcitable Kyoto type, whose conversation, no matter what was said to her, seldom went beyond one amiable sentence. Her lack of spirit went badly with Misako's own Tokyo briskness, but, more than that, the sight of her beside the old man was to Misako insufferable. It made him seem less her father than an old lecher whom she found generally repulsive.

"I'm staying for only one act," she murmured as they stepped inside the door. The heavy, old-fashioned theater samisens, whose twanging echo assailed them in the lobby, seemed to stir her to rebellion.

How many years had it been, Kaname wondered, since he had last been to the theater the old leisurely way, escorted by a teahouse maid? As he stepped from his sandals and felt the smooth, cold wood against his stockinged feet, he thought for an instant of a time, long ago —he could have been no more than four or five—when he had gone to a play in Tokyo with his mother. He remembered how he had sat on her lap as they took a rickshaw downtown from their house in the old merchants' quarter, and how afterwards his mother had led him by the hand, padding along in his holiday sandals, as they followed the maid from the teahouse. The sensation as he stepped into the theater, the smooth, cool wood against the soles of his feet, had been exactly the same then. Old-fashioned theaters with their open, straw-matted stalls somehow always seemed cold. And he had worn a kimono that day too—how clearly it called back his childhood, that feel of the air, like a penetrating, pungent mint, slipping through the kimono to his skin, chilly but pleasant, caressing as those cool, sunny days in very early spring when the plums are in bloom. "We're late," his mother had said, and he had hurried along with his heart racing.

Today, for some reason, the pit seemed even colder than the lobby. As they moved forward along the passage used by Kabuki actors for grand entrances, Kaname and Misako felt the chill bite into their arms and legs with an almost numbing intensity. The theater was fairly large and the spectators were few, and the cold wind seemed to whistle through it as through the streets outside. Even the puppets on the stage looked forlorn, dejected; they called for one's pity as they pulled their necks deep into their robes, and the whole effect was wonderfully in harmony with the tense, sad tones of the samisens and the narrators. The pit was perhaps a third full, with the spectators clustered near the stage. The old man's half-bald head and O-hisa's shining, heavy Japanese coiffure were not hard to pick out even from the rear of the theater.

O-hisa saw them as they came down the passage. "Oh, you're here," she said in her soft Kyoto accent. She carefully piled the lunch boxes at her knee, elaborate gold-flecked tiers of them, and moved back to make room for Misako beside the old man. "They've come," she said. He greeted them shortly and turned to concentrate again on the stage.

His cloak was an indefinite color, a shade of green it could probably have been called, lively and yet with a touch of somberness, like the costumes of the puppets, or like one of those mellow old brocades the model dilettante might have chosen for his cloak in the Middle Ages. Under it he wore a dark kimono with a fine printed pattern, and under that an inch or two of saffron showed at the sleeve. He sat leaning on his elbow against the wooden stall-railing, his left arm bent against his back so that his kimono stood out stiffly from his neck, and his round shoulders were even more marked than usual. He was always careful to cultivate in his dress and his

23

manner an impression of advanced years. "Old men should act like old men," he was fond of saying, and his choice of clothes today was apparently an application of his dictum that "old men only look older when they try to wear clothes too young for them." This constant emphasis on age rather amused Kaname. The old man was not really as old as all that. Assuming that he had married at twenty-five or twenty-six, and that his dead wife had borne Misako, her first daughter, not long after, he would be no more than fifty-six or so even now. He had, in Misako's expression, not yet "given up sex," and that rather substantiated the theory. "Being old is another of your father's hobbies," Kaname had once remarked to her.

"You must be uncomfortable. Why don't you stretch your legs a little this way?" O-hisa said solicitously, and busied herself in the narrow little stall making tea, pressing sweets on the others, now and then trying softly to make conversation with Misako, who disdained to look around. The old man held his saké cup lightly behind him in his outstretched right hand, balanced against the corner of an ashtray, and among her other duties O-hisa had to be sure that it was never allowed to go dry. The cup was one of three decorated in gold on vermilion with scenes from Hiroshige's prints, the old man having recently taken to insisting that "saké must be drunk from wooden lacquerware." Everything—the saké, the sweets, the cups and boxes—had been brought from Kyoto; with just such an assortment of gold-flecked lacquer, one could imagine, court maidens set out long ago to view the cherry blossoms. The old man, so particular to bring his own supplies, was not a guest to make the theater teahouses prosper, and clearly it was an effort for O-hisa to plan such expeditions.

"Won't you have some too?" O-hisa took another cup from a drawer and handed it to Kaname.

"Thank you. I never drink in the daytime. . . . It is a little chilly, though. Possibly I should have just a swallow."

She leaned to pour for him, and a suggestion of something like cloves seemed to come from her high, upswept hair as it touched against his cheek. He stared down into the cup at the gold-embossed Fuji, now shining through

24

the saké, at the tiny village below it, done in the quick style of the color prints, and at the characters indicating which was the roadside station represented.

"It makes me a little uncomfortable to drink out of anything so elegant."

"Really?" One of the traditional charms of the Kyoto beauty, the discolored teeth, showed itself in O-hisa's laugh. Her two front teeth were as black at the roots as if they had been stained in the old court manner, and farther to the right an eyetooth protruded sharp enough to bite into her lip. There were many who would have seen in such a mouth a winsome artlessness, but in honesty it could not have been called beautiful. Misako was of course being cruel when she pronounced it filthy and barbarous. To Kaname it seemed rather a little sad. That such an unhealthy mouth should be left uncared for suggested something of the woman's ignorance.

"You brought all this from home with you?" he asked O-hisa.

"We did indeed."

"And you'll have to carry all the boxes back? I sympathize with you."

"He says the food at theaters is inedible."

Misako glanced back at them, then quickly turned to the stage again. Kaname had noticed how sharply she pulled herself away when in her efforts to find a comfortable position one of her feet brushed against his knee. He could not help smiling, a little wryly, at the trial it it was for them to be put together in such a small space.

"How do you like it?" he asked in a husbandly way, hoping to dispel the mood a little.

"You must have so much excitement," O-hisa put in. "I should think you might like a nice quiet play now and then."

"I've been watching the singers. They're really much more interesting than the puppets," said Misako.

The old man coughed somewhat threateningly. His eyes still fixed on the stage, he groped about his knee for his pipe. The tooled-leather case had slipped under the cushion, however, and he was still feeling blindly for it when O-hisa noticed and retrieved it for him. She filled it, lighted it, and laid it carefully in the palm of his hand. Then, as if it made her want to smoke herself, she reached

25

into her sash, took out an amber-red leather case, and pushed her small white hand in under the lid.

There was much to be said for seeing a puppet play with a bottle of saké at one's side and a mistress to wait on one, Kaname thought as the conversation quieted and, for want of anything more to distract him, he turned his attention to the stage. The first act of *Love Suicide* was drawing to a close. The lovers, Jihei and the geisha Koharu, held the stage, Koharu seated to the right. The saké cup had been rather a large one, and Kaname felt a little heady. Perhaps because of the glittering reflections, the stage seemed a great distance away, and it was all he could do to make out the faces and the costumes. He concentrated on Koharu. Jihei's face had in it something of the dignity of classic dance masks, but his exaggerated clothes hung lifelessly from his shoulders as he moved about the stage, making it a little hard for one as unfamiliar with the puppet theater as Kaname to feel any human warmth in him. Koharu, kneeling with her head bowed, was infinitely more effective. Her clothing too was exaggerated, so that her turned-out skirt fell unnaturally before her knees, but Kaname found that easy to forget. The old man, when he discoursed on the puppet theater, liked to compare Japanese Bunraku puppets with Occidental string puppets. The latter could indeed be very active with their hands and feet, but the fact that they were suspended and worked from above made it impossible to suggest the line of the hips and the movement of the torso. There was in them none of the force and urgency of living flesh, one could find nothing that told of a live, warm human being. The Bunraku puppets, on the other hand, were worked from inside, so that the surge of life was actually present, sensible, under the clothes. Their strongest points perhaps derived from the good use made in them of the Japanese kimono. The same effects would be impossible from puppets in foreign dress, even if the same manipulating techniques were adopted. The Bunraku puppet was therefore unique, inimitable, a medium so skillfully exploited that one would be hard put to find parallels for it anywhere.

Kaname found himself agreeing. The active Jihei was ungainly, a little repulsive. That was undoubtedly because it was not possible to keep the body of the standing puppet from dangling a little and thus falling into the defects of the string puppet. If one pursued the old man's argument a little farther the kneeling puppet, it would seem, ought to have more of the "urgency of living flesh" than the standing puppet; and indeed, as she knelt there, still but for the slightest movement of the shoulders to suggest breathing, and now and then a hint of coquetry, Koharu was almost disturbingly alive. Kaname looked at his program and saw that the puppeteer was Bungorō, one of the great names in the art. His face was gentle and refined, the sort of face an accomplished artist ought to have, and he seemed to hold Koharu in his arms as he would a treasured child, smiling tranquilly down on her hair, taking such obvious pleasure in his work that one could not but feel a little envious. Suddenly Koharu seemed to Kaname like one of the fairies he had seen in *Peter Pan,* a fairy in human form but smaller, more delicate, resting in Bungorō's arms, slight against the expanse of his formal, wide-shouldered stage dress.

"I don't know much about it, but I do like Koharu," Kaname said, half to himself. O-hisa at least must have heard, but no one answered. Kaname blinked now and then in an effort to bring the stage into better focus. Presently the warmth of the saké began to clear away and Koharu emerged in sharper outline. She had been motionless for some time. Her left arm was drawn up inside her kimono, her right hand rested on a porcelain brazier, her head was sunk to her breast. As Kaname concentrated his attention on the still figure, he found that he was able to forget Bungorō, that Koharu was no longer a fairy in his arms but a live figure, kneeling solidly on the stage. Not that she was like the Koharu of one of the Kabuki actors. No matter how inspired an actor was, one still said to oneself: "That's Baikō," or, "That's Fukusuke." But here one had only Koharu herself. Her doll's features perhaps lacked the expressiveness of a Baikō or a Fukusuke, but did the geisha beauty of two centuries ago really show her emotions, her pains and her joys, as the actor does on the stage? Wasn't the real Koharu perhaps a "doll-like" woman? Whether she was or not, the ideal sought by theatergoers was surely not the Koharu of the actors but the Koharu of this puppet. The classical beauty was withdrawn, restrained, careful not to show too much

27

individuality, and the puppet here quite fitted the requirements. A more distinctive, more colorful figure would only have ruined the effect. Perhaps, indeed, to their contemporaries all the tragic heroines, Koharu and Umegawa and the rest, had the same face. Perhaps this doll was the "eternal woman" as Japanese tradition had her. . . .

Kaname had seen the Bunraku puppets once ten years before. He had not been impressed—he could in fact remember only that he had been intensely bored. Today he had come solely out of a sense of duty, expecting to be bored again, and he was somewhat astonished that he should almost against his will be drawn so completely into the play. He had grown older, he had to admit. He was no longer in a position to make fun of the old man's dilettantism. Given another ten years, he would find that he had come precisely the same distance over the same road as the old man. There he would be, a mistress like O-hisa at his side, a tooled-leather pipe-case hung at his hip, a tiered lunch box flecked with gold . . . but he might not need even ten years. He had always affected a maturity beyond his years, and he would age fast. . . . He looked at O-hisa. Her face was turned a little so that the line of her cheek showed, round, almost heavy, like that of a court beauty in a picture scroll. He compared her profile with Koharu's. Something about the slow, sleepy expression made him think of the two of them as not unlike each other. . . . A pair of conflicting emotions pressed themselves on him: old age brought its own pleasures and was not really to be dreaded; and yet that very thought, a symptom of approaching old age, was something he must resist, if only because of the advantage it might give Misako. The reason for their decision to separate, after all, was that they did not want to grow old, that they wanted to be free to live their youth again.

## CHAPTER THREE

"THANK you very much for the telephone call," Kaname said as the curtain fell and the old man turned half around to face him. "I'm beginning to see some of the good points in all this—I really am."

"You needn't try to please me. I have no professional interest in it," the old man answered, with a touch of the self-satisfaction that comes with age. His shoulders were hunched for the cold, and his neck was buried in a scarf, a piece of silk crepe, softened with age, that had once been meant for a woman. "I don't expect you to enjoy yourself, but it does you no harm to see something like this at least once in your life."

"I'm enjoying myself thoroughly, though. Why do you suppose it is?—I see a great deal I missed before."

"These are almost the last of the great puppeteers. I wonder how it will be when they are gone."

Misako cupped a small compact in the palm of her hand and began powdering her nose. "And so begins the dissertation," the expression on her face seemed to say as she bit back a sardonic smile.

"It's a shame there aren't more people to see it." Kaname looked around the theater. "I don't suppose it's so empty as this week-ends."

"On the contrary," the old man said, "this is a good crowd. The theater is just too big. The old Bunkaru was better—small and cozy."

"They won't be allowed to rebuild, the papers say."

"It's more that the company doesn't want to put any more money in. No crowds, no profits. I say this, myself: it's an Osaka art and some Osaka philanthropist ought to be willing to take care of it."

"Why don't you step up, Father?" Misako put in.

"Because I'm not from Osaka." The old man took her quite seriously. "It's Osaka's duty to look after its own art."

"But you're so fond of Osaka art. You've surrendered to Osaka."

"And by the same token, Misako, you've surrendered to foreign music?"

"Not necessarily. I do dislike this, though. Noisy."

"Noisy? Your jazz is quieter, then? I had to listen to a little of it the other day, and it's nothing more than a gang of shrine noise-makers in foreign clothes. If that's what you want, you can find any amount in Japan without bothering to import it."

"You heard it in a low-class movie theater, I suppose."

"You mean there is high-class jazz?"

"There is indeed. You don't dismiss jazz that easily."

"Really, young people are beyond me. Look at this, for instance—women have simply forgotten how to take care of themselves. What's that thing in your hand?"

"That thing is called a compact."

"A compact. I don't object so much to the fad for compacts, but I do object to the way women take them out in public, no matter who might be watching. It's inelegant, ungraceful—a woman's charm disappears. I had to scold O-hisa about it just the other day."

"A compact is very convenient." Misako turned to get a better light and, taking out a kiss-proof lipstick, solemnly drew a line of crimson across her mouth.

"But that looks so dreadful. In my day a well-bred woman would never have thought of doing such a thing in public."

"Well, everyone does now. I don't see how you're to stop it. I know a woman who is famous for making herself up at the table. Whenever we have lunch together, she takes out her compact and forgets the food. It takes forever to get through a meal. She's an extreme case, of course."

"Who's that?" Kaname asked.

"Mrs. Nakagawa. You don't know her."

"Would you do something about this, please? It seems to have burned down." The old man took a stomach-warmer, a small charcoal brazier, from his kimono and handed it to O-hisa. "The place is so big and empty, I can't seem to keep warm."

"How about something to warm you from inside?" Kaname took advantage of O-hisa's concentration on the brazier to offer the silver saké flask that had been brought with everything else from Kyoto.

Misako meanwhile was getting impatient. The curtain was about to rise, and Kaname seemed quite uninterested in finding an excuse to leave. "I don't in the least want to go, and if I can I'll get away early and meet you by seven," she had as a matter of fact said at the end of that telephone call from Suma—though she had added that she could not be sure she would succeed.

"I'll be sore all day tomorrow." She rubbed gingerly

at her knee, intensely annoyed as Kaname's glance informed her that it hardly seemed decent to leave so early.

"Why don't you sit here on the railing till the next act begins?" he suggested.

"Or you might go out and walk around the lobby," added the old man.

"Do you think I would find some excitement in the lobby?" She began bitterly, but quickly changed her manner. "I've surrendered to Osaka art even more than Father has. Only one act, and I've surrendered completely."

O-hisa chuckled.

"What do you want to do?" Misako turned to Kaname.

"It makes no difference to me." His answer was as vague as ever, but he was not able to hide a certain irritation at the way she pressed him. He knew she did not want to stay long, and he intended to withdraw gracefully when the proper time came; but they had been invited and had accepted, after all, and she ought at least for the sake of appearances to let him make the decision this once—she ought to restrain herself and play the part of the wife to that small extent.

"If we leave now, we should be just in time." Ignoring his displeasure, Misako took out her watch and flicked open the cloisonné lid, in near her sash. "I thought since we were downtown we might stop by and see what's at the Shōchiku."

"But Kaname is enjoying himself." There was a suggestion of the spoiled child in the old man's irritable frown. "You might be a little more sociable. You can go to the Shōchiku any time."

"If he wants to stay, we can stay, I suppose."

"And O-hisa spent all yesterday evening and this morning getting the lunch ready," the old man persisted. "We can't possible eat it by ourselves."

"It's nothing, really. Don't stay just for that." O-hisa had been quite outside the conversation, listening as a child would listen to grownups, but at the old man's remark she somewhat uncomfortably readjusted the lid to hide the mosaic-like array inside the square box. Even the boiling of an egg was likely to call forth a lecture from the old man, and the training of his young mistress had involved a long course in cooking. Now, however, no one

31

except O-hisa could cook a decent meal, and he was clearly anxious to show her off.

"Suppose we put off the Shōchiku till tomorrow." Kaname in his mind substituted "Suma" for "the Shōchiku." "We can stay for one more act, possibly, and sample O-hisa's feast. After that . . ." But it was clear that the gap between them had not been closed.

With the beginning of the second act, the last meeting between the ill-fated Jihei and his wife, O-san, Kaname's feelings underwent a quick change. For all that it was played by puppets with their exaggerated mannerisms, the domestic scene carried a telling authenticity that drew a wry smile from the lips of both Kaname and his wife. "Why am I left so alone? Do I nourish in my breast a serpent, a demon?" the narrator chanted for O-san, and to Kaname the line expressed, with grace and circumspection but with an acuteness that tightened his chest, the innermost secret of a marriage from which sexual passion had disappeared. He remembered vaguely that the play had been revised in the two centuries since it was first staged, but at least that line, he felt sure, must have been in the original. It was the sort of line the old man liked to seize upon when he proclaimed that the old plays contained subtleties which the modern novel could not approach. A chilling thought suddenly came to Kaname. What if the old man were to choose that very line to discourse upon? The curtain would go down and he would launch forth, with his usual missionary zeal: "They said things well in those days. 'Do I nourish in my breast a serpent, a demon?' " The possibility was a distressing one. Kaname regretted that he had not given in to Misako's wishes and left after the first act.

But presently the uneasiness vanished, and the moment came when he was again lost in the play. In the first act he had been drawn to Koharu alone, but this time he found Jihei and his wife, O-san, equally attractive. The stage was set to show the townsman's house inside its vermilion-lacquered threshold. Jihei lay back listening to his wife's supplications, his head pillowed on a square of wood and his feet tucked under a quilt against the late-autumn chill—the picture of the young man, any young man, feeling with the approach of evening a vague restlessness, a desire for the lights of the entertainment quarter. There

32

was nothing in the narrative to suggest that it was evening, but in Kaname's mind the picture was clear. There would be bats in the dusk outside the latticed window, circling over the streets of commercial, plebeian old Osaka. O-san, dressed in a subdued, wifely kimono, wore on her face, for all that it was a carved wooden face, the sadness of the unloved wife, in sharp contrast with the brightness of Koharu. It was the face of the virtuous, hard-principled townsman's wife. Now and then other characters, sometimes several of them at once, burst on the stage. The hanging, inert quality of the legs no longer bothered Kaname as it had in the first act. Indeed—how was he to account for it?—the movements of the puppets about the stage seemed completely natural.

And at the center of the shouting and wailing, the wrangling and reviling—the heavy, loud-voiced sobbing even—was Koharu, her beauty brought out in relief against the tempest she had stirred up.

Kaname began to wonder whether, in its place and done properly, the Osaka style of singing was really as coarse and noisy as he had always taken it to be. Or perhaps its very noisiness heightened the mood of tragedy. He disliked the Osaka samisen, but even more he disliked the uncouth Osaka narrator, the embodiment, it seemed to him, of certain Osaka traits that he, born and reared in Tokyo like his wife, found highly disagreeable, a sort of brashness, impudence, forwardness, a complete lack of tact when it came to pushing one's personal ends. The typical native of Tokyo has a natural reserve. Quite foreign to him is the openness of the Osakan, who strikes up a conversation with a stranger on the streetcar and proceeds—in an extreme case, it must be admitted—to ask how much his clothes cost and where he bought them. Such behavior in Tokyo would be considered outrageously rude. The plain sense of how to comport oneself is no doubt better developed in Tokyo than in Osaka. Sometimes, indeed, it is so well developed that it leads to an excessive concern with appearances and a timid unwillingness to act. But be that as it may, the son of Tokyo can, if he chooses, find in Osaka singing the perfect expression of Osaka crudeness. Surely, he may say to himself, the problem, no matter what strong emotions it stirs up, can be taken care of with less grimacing, less twisting

33

of the lips and contorting of the features, less writhing and straining toward the skies. If in fact it cannot be expressed in less emphatic and dramatic terms, then our Tokyo man is more inclined to turn it off with a joke than try to express it at all.

Misako had recently taken to practicing the Tokyo samisen to dispel her unspoken sorrows, and its clear, thin tones aroused in Kaname a feeling of pleasant intimacy mixed with regret. The old man argued that the Tokyo style was uninteresting except in the hands of a master. The amateur, he said, tended to drown out the overtones in a dead clatter as his plectrum struck the taut leather face. It was true of course that the Osaka tones were fuller, but Misako said, and Kaname agreed with her, that Japanese music was simple and one-threaded in any case, and that the lightness of the Tokyo style did not weigh it down as the grossness of the Osaka style did. When they discussed Japanese music, Kaname and Misako always formed an alliance against the old man.

The old man's arguments were full of references to "young people today." Any taste for things Occidental was found to have the same shallowness and lack of body as Occidental string puppets. What he said was never to be taken entirely at its face value, and he had himself in his earlier years indulged in foreign tastes of the most hair-raising variety. But when he heard Japanese music characterized as "one-threaded" and monotonous, he became genuinely aroused. Kaname usually found the argument not worth the effort and withdrew at a convenient juncture. It did seem unjust, though, that he should be called "shallow" because of his liking for foreign things. He had what seemed to him a profoundly good reason: pure Japanese tastes, such as the old man's, were dominated by the standards of the Edo period, the period of the two and a half centuries before the Restoration of 1868, and Kaname simply did not like the Edo period. He reacted sharply against it, but he would have been hard put to make the old man understand why. To himself he thought he could explain this antagonism very simply. Edo culture was colored through and through with the crassness of the merchant class, and no matter where one turned, one could not escape the scent of the market place. Not that Kaname found the scent an entirely repulsive one. He had grown up in the merchants' section of Tokyo before the earthquake destroyed it, and the thought of it could fill him with the keenest nostalgia; but the very fact that he was a child of the merchants' quarter made him especially sensitive to its inadequacies, to its vulgarity and its preoccupation with the material. He reacted from it toward the sublime and the ideal. It was not enough that something should be touching, charming, graceful; it had to have about it a certain radiance, the power to inspire veneration. One had to feel forced to one's knees before it, or lifted by it to the skies. Kaname required this not only in works of art. A woman-worshipper, he looked for the same divine attributes in women, but he had never come upon what he was looking for either in art or in women. He only harbored a vague dream, and its very refusal to become a reality made his longing the keener. He found in foreign novels, music, movies something that satisfied it a little, probably because of the Occidental view of women. The tradition of woman-worship in the West is a long one, and the Occidental sees in the woman he loves the figure of a Greek goddess, the image of the Virgin Mother. The attitude so pervades the customs and traditions of the West that it automatically finds expression in art and literature. Kaname had an intense feeling of loneliness and deprivation when he thought of the emotional life of the Japanese, so lacking in this particular feeling of worshipfulness. Ancient Japanese court literature and the drama of the feudal ages, with Buddhism a strong and living force behind it, had in its classical dignity something of what he sought, but with the Edo shogunate and the decline of Buddhism even that disappeared. While the dramatists and novelists of the Edo period were able to create soft, lovely women, women who were likely to dissolve in tears on a man's knee, they were quite unable to create the sort of woman a man would feel compelled to kneel before. Kaname therefore preferred a Hollywood movie to a seventeenth-century Kabuki play. For all its vulgarity, Hollywood was forever dancing attendance on women and seeking out new ways to display their beauty. And he felt that Japanese drama and music were far too much under the Edo-period influences that were so distasteful to him. Still, he could, if he tried, see a trace of a redeeming feature for the Tokyo school in the vigor and dash of the Tokyo personality. The Osaka school, to its very heart thick, coarse, heavy after the manner of the Edo period, he had always found insufferable.

Why, then, did he feel no revulsion today? Almost without his knowing it, the play had made him surrender to even the heavy Osaka accompaniment, and indeed this immoderate display of passion, precisely what one would expect from the culture of the Osaka merchant, seemed to help him a little in his own pursuit of the ideal. The lacquered threshold on the stage, the shop curtain covering part of a tapering doorway, the low, latticed partition in the foreground, all gave him a depressing sense of the moldy darkness in which the Osaka townsman lived. And yet there was in it something too of the quiet, mysterious gloom of a temple, something of the dark radiance that a Buddha's halo sends out from the depth of its niche. It was far from the brightness of a Hollywood movie. Rather it was a low, burnished radiance, easy to miss, pulsing out from beneath the overlays of the centuries.

"You must be hungry. It's nothing, really, but . . ." As the curtain fell, O-hisa began handing out the contents of the lacquer boxes.

The images of the dolls, Koharu and O-san, were still vivid in Kaname's mind. He was on edge, however, lest the old man begin his discourse on the serpent, the demon in a wife's breast, and he found it difficult to stay politely through the lunch.

"You will have to forgive us if we eat and run," Kaname said.

"Must you?"

"I'd like to stay myself, but it seems she does want to stop by the Shōchiku."

"I can understand that, but—" O-hisa looked from Misako to the old man, as if to mediate between them.

Kaname and Misako took the introduction to the last act for the proper moment to slip out. O-hisa saw them to the exit.

"We didn't have to do so very much for filial piety after all," Misako said, clearly relieved, as they came out into the lights of the theater district. Kaname did not answer. "Where are you going? It's this way."

"Oh?" He turned and followed as she started off impatiently in the other direction. "I only thought it might be easier to find a cab."

"What time do you suppose it is?"

"Six thirty."

"I wonder what I should do." She took out her gloves and tugged at them as she hurried along.

"It's still not too late, if you want to go."

"What would be the quickest? A train from Osaka station?"

"Take the electric and then a cab. We might as well say good-by here."

"What will you do?"

"Walk around a little and then go home."

"If you get home before I do, will you have someone meet me at the station around eleven? I'll probably call, though."

"Whatever you say."

Kaname stopped a new American cab for her. With a glance at her glassed-in profile, he turned back into the evening crowds.

## CHAPTER FOUR

DEAR HIROSHI:

*Are the examinations over? I expect to be there during your vacation.*

*And what shall I bring you? I have been looking for your Cantonese dog, but there doesn't seem to be one in the city. Shanghai and Canton might as well be in different countries. I have been thinking I might bring you a greyhound instead. They are very popular here. I suppose you know what a greyhound is, but I am enclosing a snapshot anyway.*

*The snapshot makes me think—maybe you would like a camera. Let me know which it is to be, a camera or a greyhound.*

*Tell your father I found his Arabian Nights at Kelly and Walsh—not the sort of Arabian Nights you yourself*

*are supposed to read, however. I have some brocade
for your mother, but my taste being what it is, I suppose
I shall be laughed at again. Tell her I have fretted much
more over her brocade than over your dog.*

*I shall have much more baggage than I can manage
by myself. If I am bringing the dog I will cable, and
possibly someone can meet the ship. It will be the*
Shanghai-maru, *in Kobe the 26th.*

TAKANATSU HIDEO

At noon on the 26th Kaname and Hiroshi were at
the ship.

"And the dog? Where is he?" Hiroshi burst out as
soon as they had found Takanatsu's cabin.

"Oh, the dog—he's outside," Takanatsu answered. He
had on a light-colored tweed jacket, a gray sweater,
and gray flannel trousers. Now and then he paused in his
work on the baggage to take a puff at a cigar, and the
concentration he lavished on it heightened the air of
bustling activity that filled the narrow little cabin.

"You seem to have brought enough baggage. How long
do you stay?" Kaname asked.

"Five or six days in this part of the country. I have
business in Tokyo too."

"What's this?"

"Shaohsin wine, very old. You can have a bottle if
you like."

"Suppose we get these small bundles out of the way.
My man's waiting below."

"But what about the dog?" Hiroshi interrupted. "Isn't
Jiiya going to take care of the dog?"

"Don't worry about that. The dog's gentle enough.
You can take care of him yourself," Takanatsu replied.

"He won't bite?"

"Absolutely not. You can do whatever you want with
him. As soon as he sees you he'll be jumping all over
you."

"What's his name?"

"Lindy. It's short for Lindbergh. A high-grade imported name."

"Did you name him?"

38

"No, he belonged to a foreigner and the name came with him."

"Hiroshi," Kaname broke in to quiet the boy, who was quite carried away with himself, "would you go below and call Jiiya, please? The cabin boy can't manage all this by himself."

Takanatsu glanced at the retreating Hiroshi, then bent to pull a bulky, heavy-looking bundle from under the bed. "He looks well enough."

"Children always look well enough. He's nervous, though. Has he said anything in his letters?"

"Not that I've noticed."

"He wouldn't, I suppose. He doesn't know exactly what's wrong, and at his age he wouldn't know what to say."

"I have noticed, though, that his letters have been coming oftener. Possibly a sign that he's upset. . . . Well, that's everything." Takanatsu sat down heavily on the bed and gave himself up to his cigar. "You haven't said anything to him yet?"

"Not yet."

"That's where I think you make a mistake, of course. But we've been over it before."

"I probably would tell him if he asked."

"Surely you don't expect him to bring the subject up first?"

"I suppose not. And so I go on not telling him."

"But that's wrong. Really it is. When the time finally does come, it will be much worse to have to break everything at once. Shouldn't you explain, with all the reasons, step by step, and make him understand what has to come?"

"He's already sensed it in a vague way. We haven't said anything directly, but we've shown enough to make him guess. He's probably resigned to the fact that something has to happen, even if he doesn't quite know what."

"But that should make it easier to tell him. . . . Look at it this way. As long as you say nothing he imagines the worst, and that's why he has a case of nerves. If he thought he might never see his mother again, wouldn't it actually relieve him to know the truth?"

"I've thought the same thing. But I dread the shock it might give him, and I go on delaying."

"I doubt if it would be the shock you think it would. Children are strong—you'd be surprised how strong. You think it would be a terrible blow to him, but you're a grownup and can't really know. The boy is growing and changing, and this is the sort of thing he takes in his stride. If you do your explaining well, he'll probably just resign himself to what can't be helped."

"I've thought over all that. I've thought over everything you've said."

The truth of the matter was that Kaname had awaited the visit of this cousin with a mixture of eagerness and dread. He was disgusted with his own indecision, his tendency to postpone action from day to week to month until it had become clear that he would not be able to speak out until a final crisis forced him to. He felt that if only Takanatsu would come, he would be pushed forward, even rudely and painfully, to a point where the elements of a solution would fall in place almost of their own accord. But now, faced with Takanatsu and what had before been only a distant possibility, he felt less encouraged than frightened, less inclined to face a decision than to recoil from it.

"What are your plans for today?" Kaname changed the subject. "Can you come directly to the house?"

"I have business in Osaka, but it can wait."

"Suppose you come and get settled first, then."

"And Misako? Is she at home?"

"She was when I left."

"Will she be waiting for me?"

"Possibly. Or possibly she'll have gone out. She's very diplomatic, and she may think it would be better to let us talk by ourselves first. Or at least she may have taken that excuse."

"I want to talk to her too, of course, but before that I'd like to find out exactly what you have in mind yourself. It's a mistake for an outsider to get mixed up in a divorce, no matter how good a friend he may be, but with you two it's a matter of getting you to make up your own minds."

"Have you had lunch?" Kaname changed the subject again.

"Not yet."

40

"Why don't we eat at the Mitsuwa, then? Hiroshi can go on ahead. He has the dog to entertain him."

"I saw him." Hiroshi burst back into the room. "He's a beauty. Just like a deer."

"You ought to see him run." Takanatsu turned toward the boy. "Faster than a train, they say. The best way to exercise him is to lead him along on a bicycle. Greyhounds run in horse races, you know."

"You must mean dog races," Hiroshi corrected.

"You have me there."

"Has he had distemper yet?"

"He's past all that, a year and seven months old. The question is how are you to get him home. A train to Osaka and then a taxi?"

"It's much easier. He can ride on the electric train all the way. Just muzzle him with something and he can go right along with the rest of us."

"We have electric cars like that now? Japan is catching up with the world."

"Oh, we have everything." Hiroshi brought a trace of the Osaka dialect into his speech.

"We have, have we." Takanatsu tried to imitate him.

"Terrible. Not a bit like Osaka."

"The boy's really become too good. He speaks a different language with Misako and me from the one he uses at school."

"I can talk with a Tokyo accent when I want to, but everyone at school is from Osaka." Hiroshi was still displaying his Osaka dialect proudly.

"Hiroshi"—Kiname interrupted the boy, who seemed prepared to run away with the conversation—"why don't you see about getting off the ship and then go along with Jiiya? Your uncle has business in Kobe."

"What are you going to do?"

"I thought I'd go along with him. It's been a long time since he's had any Kobe sukiyaki, and I thought he might like some. I don't suppose you're hungry. You had a late breakfast. And then there are some things we have to talk about."

"I see." Hiroshi knew what that meant. He looked fearfully up at his father, trying to read something from the expression on his face.

41

## CHAPTER FIVE

"IN any case, let's decide what to do about Hiroshi. It would be best to tell him, and if it's too hard for you to, I suppose I can." Takanatsu's manner of speaking was not quite impatient. He was used to acting with efficiency and dispatch, however, and he launched into the main problem as soon as they were seated in the restaurant, unable to waste even the few minutes while the sukiyaki was stewing.

"No, please don't. I should do it if anyone is to."

"You should, of course. But the point is that when the time comes you don't."

"Anyway, leave the boy to me. I know him better than anyone else—you may not have noticed the way he was behaving today."

"How was that?"

"Catching you in your mistakes, showing off his Osaka accent—he never used to be that way. He doesn't have to be so playful, no matter how well he knows you."

"I did notice that he was livelier than he needed to be. You think he was acting?"

"He was indeed."

"He thought he had to go out of his way to entertain me?"

"Partly that, I suppose. But the truth is that he's afraid of you. He likes you and at the same time he's afraid of you."

"Why should he be afraid of me?"

"He has no way of telling what an impasse we've come to, of course, but I suspect he sees your visit as a sign things are going to change. We could go on indefinitely as we are without you, but with you here, a decision may come out. Or so he probably thinks."

"And he's really not glad I came?"

"Well, you bring presents, and he likes that. He's glad to see you. He's fond of you, but he's afraid to have you come. We feel rather alike about it, I think, Hiroshi and

42

I, and that's one reason I hate to break the news to him. He doesn't want to be told any more than I want to tell him. I can see it in the way he acts. And he can't be sure what you might say. He probably knows there are things I myself would leave unsaid, and he's afraid he might have to hear them from you."

"And so he makes noise to cover his fright?"

"In a way the three of us, Misako and Hiroshi and I, are alike. We're all different, of course, but we're weak in the same way, and all of us would tend to leave things as they are. Then you come along and it seems as though we're to be forced to a decision. To tell you the truth, I'm a little afraid of you myself."

"Maybe I should wash my hands of the whole thing."

"No, not that. I'm afraid, as I say, but even so, it would be better to have the matter out finally."

"All in all, the outlook couldn't be cloudier. What about this fellow Aso? Maybe we could begin with him."

"But he's like Misako and me. He says that as long as Misako refuses to act, there's nothing he can do."

"He's right, I suppose. He could make himself look like a home-wrecker."

"We've promised to talk it over and agree on a time good for the three of us. We're to consider everyone's interests."

"But that means you will forever do nothing. Really, what can be accomplished unless one of you finally takes the initiative? Your good time will never come."

"That's not quite true. Spring vacation this month would have been a good time, for instance. One of the things holding me back has been the idea of having Hiroshi in school when the break comes. I can't stand the thought of him away by himself, completely upset, maybe breaking into tears right in class. During a vacation I can go off somewhere with him, take him to the movies. I can do something anyway to keep him occupied until the first shock passes and he begins to adjust himself."

"Why haven't you done it this month, then?"

"Because it's bad for Aso. His brother is going abroad early next month and Aso would rather not worry him with family problems while he's getting ready. It would be much better to wait till he's out of the country, Aso says."

"So that the next opportunity will be summer vacation?"

"That's right. Summer vacation is longer, too, and the chances will be better."

"And something will come up then, too, and we'll have another delay. Really, there's no end to it all." Takanatsu's hand, thin but strong-looking, heavy-veined over the knuckles, trembled slightly as though gripping something heavy. The saké was possibly having its effect. He reached over and flicked the ashes from his cigar, and they fell like heavy flakes of snow into the water around the base of the brazier.

Kaname always felt a certain unreality when he talked to this cousin, back from China every two or three months; the conversation always proceeded as though the only question were: "When is the divorce to be?" Actually the earlier question: "Will there be a divorce?" was still far from answered. Takanatsu took it as firmly decided that there was to be a divorce and worried only about the time and the method. He was not on his own initiative insisting on a divorce; it was simply that he had been called into consultation only on the question of means—the more basic question, he could assume, having already been settled. Kaname for his part was not purposely displaying a strength he did not feel; but perhaps a contagious air of strength and virility about Takanatsu stirred him to a bold enthusiasm and led him to suggest more decision than he should in honesty have allowed himself. More than that: part of the pleasure he got from Takanatsu's visits lay in the feeling they gave him of controlling his own destiny. Quite unable to take action, sunk in daydreams of what it would be like once action was finally taken, he found that Takanatsu's visits stimulated the daydreams to a pleasant new liveliness, an immediacy, as though they were about to become realities. Still, it would not be right to say that he used Takanatsu only as a sort of vehicle for turning out more vigorous daydreams. Rather he hoped that through Takanatsu the daydreams might turn into something solid.

A separation is always sad. Regardless of who is involved, there is a certain sadness in the mere fact of a separation, and Takanatsu was of course right that nothing would ever come of their waiting arm in arm for the perfect moment. There had been none of this hesitating when Takanatsu himself had left his wife. After he made up his mind he simply called her into the room one morning and informed her, and spent the rest of the day explaining his reasons. And when it was settled, they lay in each other's arms all night, the final parting before them —"She cried, and I cried—I wailed, too," Takanatsu told Kaname later. Kaname had come to Takanatsu with his problem because the latter had been through the experience and because Kaname had watched with some envy the firmness he had shown. Kaname could tell himself that the sort of man who could face sorrow squarely and who could weep as the situation demanded was more composed when the crisis had passed—that, indeed, without some such ability one could not make a break at all. But Kaname was not up to following the example. He was guided by a Tokyo-bred sense of how to comport himself, and with his dislike for the unrestrained Osaka drama he could only with revulsion see himself as the contorted, weeping principal in a scene from an Osaka melodrama. He wanted to carry through cleanly, without disfiguring tears. He wanted the decision to be as though he and his wife had arrived at it in complete harmony, their separate feelings melted into a general, embracing consent.

And he did not think that was impossible. His case was after all not like Takanatsu's. He had nothing against his wife. They simply did not excite each other. Everything else—their tastes, their ways of thinking—matched perfectly. To him she was not "female," to her he was not "male"—it was the consciousness of being husband and wife and yet not being husband and wife that caused the tension between them, and had they not been married they could probably have been excellent friends.

Kaname felt, indeed, that there was no reason why he need stop seeing her after they had separated. He saw no reason why, with the passage of the years, he could not meet her pleasantly and without rancor as the wife of Aso and the mother of Hiroshi. When the time came, of course, it might not be so easy to do, out of deference to Aso and public opinion, as it seemed now, but the sorrow and regret which the simple word "parting" carried with it would be lessened he did not know how much if they parted with at least the intention of seeing each other again. Misako had once said: "You will let me know, won't you, if Hiroshi is ever seriously ill?—you must promise me you will. I should hate to think I couldn't see him. Aso says he wouldn't mind." Kaname felt sure that "Hiroshi" included "Hiroshi's father," and he of course wanted similar permission from her. They had not been entirely happy perhaps, but they had after all lived together as husband and wife, gone to bed together and got up together, for more than ten years, had even had a child together. Was there a law requiring that once they parted they must be to each other as strangers passing in the street, that if the worst came they might not even meet at one or the other's deathbed? If as time went by they acquired new mates and new children, the desire to see each other might fade, but at least for the present the reservation with which they would part was the best comfort they had.

"As a matter of fact, there's another point. You may laugh, but it wasn't only because of the boy that I wanted to make the break this month."

"Oh?" Takanatsu looked questioningly at Kaname, whose eyes had fallen to the brazier and whose lips were curled slightly in an uncomfortable smile.

"I spoke of a time that's good for all of us, but one of the things I wanted to consider was the season. Some seasons would be so much sadder than others. It would be hardest to separate in the fall. Much the saddest time of the year. I know a man who was all ready for a final break, and then his wife broke into tears and told him to take care of himself with the winter coming on, and he canceled the whole thing. I can see how that might happen."

"Who was it?"

"No one in particular. I heard the story somewhere."

"You seem to go about gathering examples."

"I keep wondering how other people managed. I don't especially go around asking, but I seem naturally to hear of every sort of case. But then ours is rather an unusual one and there aren't many precedents that help."

46

"The best time of the year, then, is when it's warm and sunny, like now?"

"That's my theory. It's still a little chilly but it's getting warmer, and before long the cherry blossoms will be out and after that the new leaves—everything to make a separation as easy as it could be."

"Have you come to this conclusion by yourself?"

"Misako agrees. If we're to separate, it should be in the spring."

"Splendid. That means, I suppose, that now you have to wait till next spring."

"Summer wouldn't be too bad . . . but my mother died in the summer. July. I can remember it so well. Everything should have been warm and alive, but summer that year was sadder than I'd ever thought it could be. The sight of green leaves made me choke up with tears. There was nothing I could do."

"You see, then? It makes no difference whether it's the spring or any other time of the year. If something happens while the cherries are in bloom, you choke up when you see cherry blossoms."

"I've wondered myself if that might not be true. But if I let myself think so, my chance goes and I find myself with no hope at all."

"And you might end up by not getting a divorce?"

"Do you think so?"

"The question is: do you?"

"I honestly don't know. The only thing I know is that the reasons for getting a divorce are all too clear. We didn't get on well before, and certainly we can't go on being married to each other—we really aren't any more —now that this affair with Aso has developed. Or I should say now that I've encouraged her into it. That's all I really know. Misako knows it too, but we can't make a decision between being sad for a little while and being wretched for the rest of our lives. Or rather we've made the decision and have trouble finding the courage to carry it through."

"Suppose you think of it this way: if you're no longer married anyway, then it's only a question of whether you go your own ways or not—a question of whether you go on living in the same house or not. Might that make it easier?"

"I've tried that. But it isn't as easy as you'd think."

"Because of Hiroshi? It's not as if he'd have to stop calling Misako his mother, though."

"I suppose it's a common enough thing for families to be separated. In the civil service the father has to live abroad or in the provinces and leave the children in Tokyo. And in the country where there are no schools, children have to live away from home. I could think of it that way if I had to."

"You're telling yourself how sad it all is. Really it isn't so sad as you let yourself think."

"But, after all, sorrow is a very subjective thing. The real trouble is that Misako and I have no resentment against each other. If we did, it would be easier, but each of us thinks the other is perfectly right, and that makes everything impossible."

"It might have been best if they'd grabbed the reins and eloped."

"As a matter of fact, before we found ourselves in this tangle Aso apparently suggested that. But Misako laughed and said she couldn't possibly do it unless he gave her ether and carried her away unconscious."

"How would it be if you were to work up a quarrel?"

"No good. We would know we were acting. 'Get out,' I'd say. 'I'm going,' she'd answer, and when it actually came to doing it, one or the other would break into tears."

"A problem couple if there ever was one. Deciding to get a divorce and then putting every possible obstacle in the way."

"It would be good if there were some sort of mental anesthetic you could take. . . . How was it when you left Yoshiko? You were able to hate her, I suppose."

"I did feel some resentment, but I felt a great deal of regret at the same time. I doubt if it's really possible to hate anyone except another man."

"But—this will sound strange, I know—don't you suppose it's easier to divorce a woman with a past? She doesn't take the matter too seriously, and she's known plenty of men before you and can go happily back to her old life."

"You probably wouldn't say so if you'd had the experience." Takanatsu's face clouded slightly, but he quickly recovered and went on in his brisk manner: "It's probably like your seasons. There's no type of woman it's easier to leave than any other type."

"I wonder if that's true. I've always thought the courtesan type—could you call it?—would be easy to leave and the other type hard—the mother type. Maybe I'm thinking only of my own problem, though."

"But the very fact that a divorce means so little to your 'courtesan type' makes it in a way sadder. Then, too, if she arranges herself a good marriage it's another thing, but if she goes back to the gay life, it reflects on you somehow. I'm quite past it all myself, of course, but you can't say it's easy to leave either a loose woman or a prim one."

The conversation died and they turned to the food for a time. They had drunk very little, but the slight flush of intoxication persisted surprisingly, and with it a heavy, springlike drowsiness.

"Shall we have dessert?"

"All right." Kaname turned moodily to press the button.

"I suppose, as a matter of fact," Takanatsu began again, "all women these days have a little of the courtesan in them. Misako herself isn't a pure maternal type."

"Oh, but she is, though, basically. It's just that she's covered it over lately with a coating of the other."

"You may be right. The matter of the coating is important. It's got so that to some extent every woman tries to make herself look like an American movie star and naturally takes on a little the look of your courtesan. It's happening in Shanghai too."

"I can't say I haven't tried to push Misako in that direction."

"Because you're a woman-worshipper. Woman-worshippers prefer the courtesan to the mother."

"That's not quite the point. The point is—what shall I say?—to go back a little, I've tried to push her in that direction because I've thought the courtesan type would be easier to leave. But it hasn't helped. If she really had changed through and through, it might have worked out as I hoped, but she has only a thin covering and at the crucial moment the metal underneath always shows through and makes everything seem more impossible than ever."

"What does she think?"

"She says she's degenerated—she's not so plain and decent as she once was. It's true, of course, but at least half the fault is mine."

A new thought came to Kaname, and with it he seemed to see himself displayed in all his chilly inhumanity. In the years since he married Misako he had been obsessed with one question: how to leave her. "I must get away, I must get away"—it was as though he had married for that one purpose. He had told himself, however, that though he could not love her, he could at least treat her with respect. But if this was not the most unmixed contempt, what could be? What woman, maternal type or wanton type, lively and sociable or reserved and withdrawn, could bear the cold loneliness of being married to such a man?

"I wouldn't object if she honestly were a courtesan," Kaname finally added.

"I'm not so sure of that either. Do you think you could tolerate the sort of thing Yoshiko did?"

"That's beside the point. Forgive me for saying so, but I wouldn't consider marrying a woman who's actually been a professional. I've never taken to geisha. What I have in mind is a smart, intelligent modern woman with something of the courtesan in her."

"And would you like it then if she played the courtesan after you were married?"

"She would be intelligent, I said. She would have some self-restraint."

"You are being very demanding indeed. Where, I wonder, will we find the woman to satisfy you? You really should have stayed single—all woman-worshippers should be single. They never find the woman who answers all the requirements."

"One try at it has been enough. I'll not get married again—for a while at least—maybe for the rest of my life."

"You'll marry again and make a mess of it again. All woman-worshippers do."

The waitress came with dessert and interrupted the conversation.

## CHAPTER SIX

IT was nearly ten. Misako lay in bed listening drowsily to the sounds from the garden outside. Hiroshi seemed to be playing with the new dog: "Lindy, Lindy," and "Peony, Peony," over and over again. Peony was a fe-male collie they had bought the year before from a Kobe kennel, and she owed her smart English name to the fact that the peony bed had been in bloom when she arrived.

"You can't do it that way." It was Takanatsu's voice. "You can't get them to be friends so soon. Leave them alone and they'll make up to each other in their own time."

"But I thought a male and a female weren't supposed to fight." That was Hiroshi.

"He only came yesterday. Give him time."

"Which do you suppose would win if they did have a fight?"

"Which would, I wonder. The trouble is that they're so nearly the same size. If one were smaller, the other would ignore him and they'd be friends in no time."

One of the dogs barked and then the other in alternation. Misako had not yet seen the new dog. She had come home late the evening before and had talked to Takanatsu, half asleep from the strain of travel, no more than twenty minutes or a half-hour. The hoarse, woolly bark probably belonged to the collie, she decided. Misako was not so fond of dogs as Kaname and Hiroshi were, but this Peony was a little different. When she came home late at night, Peony was always at the station with Jiiya, ready to leap at her with a joyful ringing of its chain, and she would scold Jiiya as she wiped the dirt from her kimono. Gradually she had lost her dislike for the dog, until sometimes now in an affectionate mood she would pat its head and feed it milk. Jumped upon as usual last night at the station, she had said with a friendly pat: "You got yourself a new playmate today, didn't you?" Peony was always the first and gladdest to see her, a

51

sort of special emissary from her husband's house, it almost seemed.

The shutters had been left closed to let Misako sleep late. She could tell from the light coming through above them that it was a bright, warm day, the sort of day that made one think of peach blossoms and the Doll Festival. She wondered whether she would have to get out all those dolls and arrange them on their tiered stand again this year. Always fond of festival dolls, her father had ordered a set in the old style from Kyoto shortly after she was born, and she had brought them along in her trousseau. She would as soon leave them buried in their closet if the choice were hers, since she had no daughters and she was not the sort to go through old routines for their own sake. The difficulty was that her father was so near. Each year when April came he was taken with a sentimental yearning for the dolls and hurried down from Kyoto to see them. He had done so last year and the year before, and he most probably would this year too. It was not the prospect of dragging all the boxes from the closet and wiping away a year's dust that bothered her —that she could stand well enough. It was rather the thought of another ordeal like the recent one at the theater. Could she avoid bringing them out this year, she wondered. Maybe she should talk the matter over with Kaname. And what would happen to the dolls when she left this house for good? Would she take them with her? She could leave them with Kaname, but that might not be pleasant for him. . . .

Her mind ran thus uncertainly to the future because it was quite possible that she would no longer be here when the Doll Festival came. But even in bed she could sense the brightness of the spring morning, and she felt alive and happy. She lay for a time on her back, her head high on the pillow, looking at the light over the shutters. For the first time in weeks she had had enough sleep. The drowsiness fast going, she found it pleasant to stretch her arms and legs under the quilt, clinging greedily to the warmth. Hiroshi's empty bed was next to hers, and Kaname's by the alcove beyond. An emerald-colored vase in the alcove over Kaname's pillow held a branch of two of camellias.

They had this guest named Takanatsu, she knew,

and she should be up and about, entertaining him, but it was so rare that she had the luxury of sleeping late in the morning. Hiroshi had always slept between her and Kaname, and when one of them had to get up in the morning and see him off to school, Misako usually let Kaname sleep. On Sunday mornings, when there was no school, she would have enjoyed staying in bed herself, but even then Hiroshi was up at seven or so and she felt she ought at least to make a gesture toward looking after him. She had to consider too the fact that she had started putting on weight these last two or three years. It was not good to allow herself too much sleep. Still, there was nothing quite like the pleasure of staying in bed late, and indeed she wondered occasionally whether she might not be getting too little sleep. Her attempts to sleep in the daytime were never as successful as they might be, however. The sleeping medicine she sometimes took in the afternoon only made her more alert and wakeful than ever. Once a week Kaname had to show his face at the office in Osaka, and sometimes, perhaps twice or three times a month, perhaps not that often, he would have a fit of helpfulness and see Hiroshi off to school himself. In any case, whether to sleep or not, it was a very rare thing for her to have the bedroom to herself.

The commotion outside, the barking and Hiroshi's voice, had about it the feel of spring and made her think of the tranquil, soft skies they had had the last three or four days. She would have to talk to Takanatsu today, of course, but that thought upset her only as much as the earlier thought of the festival dolls had. If she let everything upset her, there would be no end to her wretchedness. She wanted always to be in spirits as bright as the skies today, and she wished she could meet every problem with the casual, unhurried eye one has for festival dolls. Presently she gave way to a child-like curiosity about the dog Lindy and turned to get out of bed.

"Good morning." She opened one shutter and called out in a voice quite capable of competing with Hiroshi's.

"Good morning," Takanatsu answered. Hiroshi was busy with the dogs. "How much longer do you intend to sleep?"

"What time is it?"

"Twelve noon."

"You lie. It's no more than ten."

"But how can you sleep on such a beautiful morning?" Misako laughed. "It's a beautiful morning for sleep, too."

"But the important thing is that you're being rude to your honored guest," Takanatsu countered.

"Oh, him. He's no guest. There's nothing at all to worry about."

"I forgive you. Brush your teeth and come on out. I have something for you too." Takanatsu's face as he looked up at the window was partly hidden by a branch of plum blossoms.

"That's the new dog?"

"That's the new dog. They're very popular in Shanghai these days."

"Isn't he a beauty, Mother?" Hiroshi spoke for the first time. "Uncle Hideo says you ought to go out walking with this sort of dog."

"And what reason does he give?"

"Foreign women use dogs as a sort of ornament," Takanatsu answered. "Go out with him and you'll look more beautiful than ever."

"Even I will look beautiful?"

"I guarantee it."

"But he's so thin. I'd look plumper than I am."

"That would be nice for the dog, wouldn't it? 'She sets me off so beautifully,' he'd be saying."

"I won't forget that remark."

Hiroshi joined in the laughter, whether he understood or not.

There were five or six large plum trees in the garden, left from what had been a farm orchard when this suburb was still open country. The first blossoms came out early in February, followed through to the end of March by one branch after another. Even now, when most of the petals had fallen, there was still a dot of the purest white here and there in the bright sunlight. Peony and Lindy were tethered to the trunks, just far enough apart so that they could not spring on each other. Apparently tired of barking, they lay like a pair of glowering sphinxes. Misako could not see very clearly through the plum branches, but Kaname seemed to be sitting in a rattan chair on the veranda of the Western-style wing. He had a teacup in his hand and was flicking over the pages of a large book. Takanatsu had taken a chair out to the edge of the garden, where he sat with a cloak thrown over his night kimono, his long underwear showing untidily at the heels.

"Leave your dogs there. I'll be right down."

She came out on the veranda after a quick morning bath.

"Have you eaten?"

"Of course. We waited and waited, but you showed no sign of getting up." Kaname took a sip from the teacup in his right hand and turned his attention back to the book.

"Would you care for a bath, madame?" said Takanatsu. "The lady of the house does nothing for her guests, but the maids are wonderful. They got up early this morning and heated the bath specially. If you don't mind going in after me, why don't you have a bath yourself?"

"I've had one—I didn't realize it was after you, of course."

"It must have been a quick one."

"Do you suppose it's all right?"

"What?"

"Going in after you. I won't catch any dreadful Chinese diseases?"

"You're joking. It would be better to worry about what you might catch from Kaname here."

"I stay quietly at home." Kaname looked up from the book again. "It's you foreigners we need to watch."

"Mother," Hiroshi called from the garden, "aren't you coming out to look at him?"

"I don't mind looking at him, but you and your dogs managed to wake me early this morning. And Hideo right in with you, shouting at the top of your lungs, practically from daybreak."

"I'm a businessman, you know. You perhaps wouldn't guess it from looking at me. In Shanghai I get up every morning at five and go for a gallop out Szechuan Road before work."

"You still ride?" Kaname asked.

55

"I certainly do. No matter how cold the morning is, I don't feel right until I've had my ride."

"Couldn't you bring the dog over here?" Kaname, reluctant to leave the sunny veranda, called to them as they started out into the garden.

"Hiroshi, boy," Misako called out to him, "your father says to bring the dog over here."

Hiroshi seemed to be having trouble. "Lindy!" The branches of the far plum tree began to rustle, and Peony's hoarse bark rang out. "Quiet, Peony, quiet. Will someone come and get Peony? She's making a nuisance of herself."

"Down, Peony." Takanatsu came over with the collie, and Misako climbed hastily to the veranda as the dog threatened to jump up and lick her cheek.

"You're much too affectionate, Peony. Really, Hiroshi, you should have left her where she was."

"But she was making so much noise."

"Dogs are very jealous animals." Takanatsu squatted at the foot of the stairs beside Lindy, rubbing the palm of his hand over its throat.

"Have you found a tick?" Kaname asked.

"I've made a discovery."

"A discovery?"

"Come and feel this. It's most remarkable."

"Do tell us what's remarkable."

"When you feel it here like this, it's exactly like a human being's." Takanatsu rubbed his own throat and then the dog's again. "Come and feel it, Misako. I'm not lying."

"Let me feel it." Hiroshi ran over ahead of his mother. "You're right. You really are. Let me feel Mother's now."

"Oh, please," Misako protested. "Is it nice to put your mother and a dog in the same class?"

"What does she mean, 'Is it nice?' Why, Hiroshi, your mother can't compete with this dog. If she had a skin as smooth as this she'd be too conceited to talk to us."

"Suppose you come feel my throat, sir."

"In a minute, in a minute. You come feel the dog's throat first. See? What did I tell you? Isn't it strange?"

"Hmm. Very strange indeed. You're quite right. Don't you want to feel it too?" she called to Kaname.

"Where, where?" Kaname came down from the veranda. "Well, so it is. Most remarkable. It gives you a strange feeling, doesn't it?"

"You credit me with a new discovery?"

"The hair is so short and silky it hardly feels like hair at all," Kaname mused.

"And the neck is just the right size, too. I wonder which of us has a bigger neck." Misako cupped one hand against the dog's throat and the other against her own. "His is bigger. It's because he's so long and thin that it looks smaller."

"Exactly my size," said Takanatsu.

"Collar fourteen and a half," added Kaname.

"And so whenever I get lonesome for you I can come out and feel the dog's throat."

"Uncle Hideo! Uncle Hideo!" Hiroshi called into Lindy's ear.

"So you're changing his name from Lindy to Uncle Hideo? How about it, boy?" Kaname laughed.

"Really, Hideo," said Misako, "I'm sure there must be places where this dog would be much more welcome than here."

"What do you mean?"

"You don't understand? And it's so clear to me. There must be someone who would spend her whole day rubbing the dog's throat and thinking of you."

"Maybe you brought it here by mistake?" Kaname suggested.

"You people are impossible. Right in front of the child, too. No wonder he's so brash."

"That reminds me, Father," Hiroshi broke in. "I heard something good when we were bringing Lindy back from Kobe."

"Oh? And what did you hear?"

"Jiiya and I were walking along the Bund, and a drunk—I think he must have been drunk—came after us watching Lindy. 'An amazing dog,' he kept saying. 'Exactly like a conger eel.' "

They all laughed.

"He has a point, you know," said Takanatsu. "The dog does remind you a little of a conger eel. Lindy, you old conger eel!"

"Maybe we can call him Conger Eel," said Kaname,

as if debating the matter with himself. "And so, by grace of the conger eel, Uncle Hideo will be spared."

"They have the same sort of longish face, don't they, Peony and Lindy," said Misako.

"Collies and greyhounds have the same faces and the same bodies too," Takanatsu answered. "Only one has long hair and the other short—I add this for the benefit of those who do not know as much about dogs as I do."

"And their throats?"

"Let's drop the throats. That doesn't seem to have been a happy discovery."

"Lined up side by side at the foot of the stairs, they remind you a little of the main Mitsukoshi store, don't they?"

"The Mitsukoshi? Does the Mitsukoshi have two dogs, Mother?"

"Shocking. Your son is a Tokyo man and he doesn't even know about the lions at the Mitsukoshi. That, I suppose, explains why his Osaka accent is so good."

"But I was only six when I left Tokyo."

"I almost think you're right. Time does fly. And you haven't been back since?"

"I always want to go, but Father runs off and leaves me here with Mother."

"Why don't you go with me? You're having a vacation. . . . I'll show you the Mitsukoshi."

"When?"

"Tomorrow. The day after, maybe."

"I wonder if I should." Hiroshi had been chattering along happily, but a shadow passed over his face.

"Why don't you go with him, Hiroshi?" Kaname suggested.

"I'd like to, I suppose. But there's my homework."

"And haven't I been telling you to get your homework done early?" Misako reminded him. "Work hard at it all day today and you'll have it finished. Then you can ask your uncle to take you to Tokyo with him. Doesn't that seem a fine idea?"

"We won't worry about homework. We can get that done on the train. I'll even help."

"How long will you be in Tokyo?"

"I'll get you back in time for school."

58

"Where are you going to stay?"

"At the Imperial Hotel."

"But won't you have all sorts of work to do?"

"Imagine the child arguing about it when his uncle offers to take him to Tokyo. Do take him along, Hideo, even if he's a nuisance. It will be so peaceful without him for a few days."

Hiroshi looked into his mother's eyes as she spoke. He was still smiling, but his face seemed a little pale. The thought of taking him along to Tokyo had come to Takanatsu quite on the spur of the moment, but Hiroshi found another explanation: they had planned it in advance. If they really wanted only to give him pleasure, then of course he had no objection to being taken to Tokyo. But he dreaded what Takanatsu might say to him on the train back. "Hiroshi, you will find your mother gone. Your father asked me to talk to you about it" —might he not have to hear something like that? The boy stood before them in a torment of uncertainty, trying to guess what was going on in their grown-up minds, frightened and at the same time vaguely aware that he was perhaps being childish.

"You do not have to go to Tokyo? You have business there?"

"Why?"

"If you don't, you can stay here. I'd like that better. It would be more fun for all of us. Mother and Father too."

"Can't they be satisfied with Lindy? They can feel his throat every day."

"But Lindy can't talk to them the way you can. Can you, Lindy? You can't take the place of Uncle Hideo, can you, Lindy?" Hiroshi squatted beside the dog, stroking its throat and rubbing his cheek against its side to cover his confusion. Something about his voice and manner made them suspect that he was crying.

But whatever sorrows and dangers they faced, it seemed to be the rule that Misako and Kaname could laugh and joke when Takanatsu was with them as they could not by themselves. That may have been partly the result of his efforts to put them at ease, but what really seemed to lift the weight from their spirits was the fact that Takanatsu alone knew everything, that there was no need to act in front of him. How long had it been, Misako wondered, since she had last heard Kaname really laugh. The peace and calm of being able to sit on a sunny south veranda, chair opposite chair, watching the boy and the dogs at play in the garden below—the contentment of receiving this visitor from afar, Kaname speaking, Misako answering, the reserve between them broken down—showed unexpectedly how much there still was about them of the husband and wife when for the moment they were free not to play at being husband and wife. It would not last, they knew, but they could enjoy breathing freely for one short moment.

"How's the literature? You seem carried away."

"It's very, very interesting." Kaname was lost again in the book that had lain face down on the table before him. He held it high in front of his face, but even so the others caught a glimpse of a full-page copperplate teeming with naked harem ladies.

"I don't know how many trips I had to make to Kelly and Walsh to get that for you. I heard they finally had it in from England and ran around to buy it. But the rascal probably saw how much I wanted it and asked two hundred dollars. Wouldn't come down a cent. He had the cheek to tell me I couldn't find another set even in London and I was a fool to expect a discount. I know nothing about the book market, but I pushed away at him, and finally he came down ten per cent and made me pay cash on the spot."

"It's as expensive as that?" asked Misako.

"But it's not just one volume," Kaname explained. "Seventeen all together."

"And those seventeen volumes were a problem too. It's classed as obscene, and it's full of illustrations that give it away. I thought customs might be embarrassing if I got caught with seventeen obscene volumes, so I put all seventeen in my trunk. Which was all right, except then my trunk was practically immovable. You've no idea how I labored for those books. Most people would expect a fat commission." Takanatsu used English words like "obscene" and "illustrations."

"It's different from my *Arabian Nights?*" Hiroshi had not entirely understood what Takanatsu was talking about, but his curiosity was aroused. He cast an eager eye at the book, trying to get a glimpse of the illustration under his father's hand.

"In places it's the same and in places different. The *Arabian Nights* is for grown-ups, but there are some stories that are all right for you. Those are the ones in the *Arabian Nights* you have."

"Is Ali Baba in it?"

"He is."

"And Aladdin's lamp?"

"It is."

"And 'Open Sesame'?"

"It is—all the ones you know are there."

"Is it hard to read in English? How many days will it take you, Father?"

"I've no intention of reading the whole thing. I pick out the interesting spots and read them."

"Even so, I'm filled with admiration. I've forgotten practically all the English I ever knew. No occasion to use it except sometimes in business," said Takanatsu.

"But this sort of book is different. You want to read it even if you have to have a dictionary in one hand."

"That's for men of leisure. Poor men like me can never find the time."

"Strange," Misako put in. "I heard somewhere that you were *nouveau riche.*"

"I made some money just in time to lose it again."

"A pity. How did you lose it?"

"On the dollar market."

"Speaking of dollars, let me pay you before I forget. How much does a hundred and eighty dollars come to?" Kaname asked.

"But you don't have to pay, do you? Isn't it a present?"

"A present!" Takanatsu was outraged. "The woman is talking nonsense. Do people bring presents that cost a hundred and eighty dollars? I brought this because I was ordered to."

"And what about my present?"

"Oh, your present. I forgot about that. Let's go in and have a look. You can pick out one you like."

Misako and Takanatsu went up to Takanatsu's room on the second floor of the foreign wing.

## CHAPTER SEVEN

"WHAT a dreadful smell!"

As they came into the room, Misako began fanning the air with her kimono sleeve. Her face buried in her arm, she hurried around to open the windows.

"A dreadful smell, really—you still eat the stuff?"

"I do. And then I smoke expensive cigars to cover up."

"But it's even worse all mixed up with tobacco smoke. The room is a horror. If you must go about making smells like this, I shall have to ask you to return the nightgown I lent you."

"It'll wash right out. No trouble at all. Besides, if I were to take it off and return it now, the damage would already be done."

It had not been so noticeable outside in the garden, but here in the tight Western-style room the combined smell of garlic and tobacco, stagnant through the night and morning, assaulted the nose with a strangling intensity.

"You have to follow the Chinese and eat lots of garlic. Then you don't catch Chinese diseases." That was one of Takanatsu's favorite theories, and he never passed a day in Shanghai without his garlic-loaded Chinese food. "It doesn't seem like Chinese food," he was fond of adding, "unless it smells of garlic." Always when he came back to Japan he had a supply of dried garlic with him, and he took slivers of it like a habitual tonic. Besides strengthening his stomach's defenses, he said, it gave him energy, and he was quite unable to do without it. "His wife ran away because he reeked of garlic," Kaname liked to say.

"I should be forever grateful if you would stand just a bit farther off."

"Hold your nose if you don't like it." Takanatsu puffed away at a cigar he held in one hand while with the other he opened his suitcase out flat on the bed. The suitcase was battered to a point where one could have given it to a ragpicker with few regrets.

"What a supply! You look like a clothes-peddler."

"I have to give some presents in Tokyo this time. Do you see any you like? But I suppose I'll be sneered at again."

"How many can I have?"

"Two, possibly three. . . . How would this one be?" Takanatsu took out one of the strips of brocaded sash cloth.

"It's much too drab."

"Too drab is it? How old are you? The man said it would suit a girl or a married woman of maybe twenty-two or three."

"But you can't trust a Chinese salesman on things like that."

"It's a store where a great many Japanese go, and he should be well up on Japanese tastes. My woman, as a matter of fact, always asks his advice."

"Well, it's not the sort of thing I would buy. And the material's not as good as it might be. Mohair, isn't it?"

"You have your eye on the other, I see. Well, if you have to have the satin, I can only let you have two. You can have three of the mohair."

"I'll take the satin, thank you. Two satin are better than three mohair. How about this one, for instance?"

"That one?"

"What do you mean, 'That one'? Do you have other plans for it?"

"I was saving that one for the youngest of the girls in Tokyo."

"Oh, no! Poor Suzuko could never wear this. You amaze me."

"On the contrary, you amaze me. Put on these gay robes and you'll look like a loose woman."

"Oh, but I am a loose woman."

Takanatsu regretted his remark as soon as he had made it, but Misako's show of candor turned it off smoothly.

"A lamentable slip of the tongue. This member was in error and would like to retract his statement. He requests that it be stricken from the verbatim record."

"Too late. It's already in the record."

"This member had no malicious intent. He apologizes most humbly for having sullied the reputation of a pure woman and for having disturbed the order of the session."

"She's not such a pure woman, you know," Misako laughed.

"It's all right then not to retract?"

"It doesn't make much difference—it's a reputation that rather tends to get itself sullied anyway."

"Come, now. I thought special pains were being taken to see that it did not."

"So Kaname says, but it seems useless to me. Did you talk about it yesterday?"

"Yes."

"What does he think?"

"It was all as usual very vague and not much to the point."

They sat one at each end of the bed, the suitcase and its overflow of bright cloth between them.

"And what do you think yourself?" Takanatsu asked.

"What do I think? I can't really tell you in a word."

"Take two or three words."

"Do you have anything to do today?"

"I'm quite free. I purposely took care of all my business in Osaka yesterday so that today would be open."

"What does Kaname have planned?"

"He said he thought he would take Hiroshi to maybe an amusement park this afternoon."

"Let's get Hiroshi's homework done. You will take him to Tokyo, won't you?"

"I'd just as soon, but he seemed so upset. Wasn't he crying?"

"He certainly was. He's that way. . . . To tell you the truth, what I want to do is see how I get along without him. Two or three days even would be enough for a trial."

"That seems like not a bad idea. And in the meantime you could have things out with Kaname."

"I'm afraid not. I'll have to ask you to tell me what Kaname thinks. When the two of us are alone face to face, we simply are not able to say what we would like to. We go on well enough to a point, but beyond that one or the other of us is sure to break down in tears."

"It's fairly definite, is it, that you can go to Aso's?"

"Quite definite. The only problem is making up our minds to it."

"Do you suppose his family knows?"

"In a vague sort of way they seem to."

"How much?"

"That I am seeing Aso now and then with Kaname's permission. That much they probably know."

"And pretend they don't?"

"Very probably. There's not much else they could do."

"And if matters were to go further?"

"I don't think there would be any difficulty once Kaname and I were cleanly separated. Aso says his mother understands perfectly how he feels."

The barking began again in the garden below. The dogs had resumed their feud.

"More of that!" Misako threw down the cloth she had been fingering in her lap and went over to the window. "Hiroshi, suppose you take the dogs over there. We can't talk for the noise."

"I was just going to."

"Where's your father?"

"On the veranda. He's still reading."

"How would it be if you stopped playing and began your homework?"

"Where's Uncle Hideo?"

"You needn't wait for him. Uncle Hideo, you say, as though he had come specially to see you."

"But he said he'd help me with my homework."

"He will not. What is homework for if you're not to do it yourself?"

"I see." They could hear Hiroshi clattering off with the dogs.

"He seems more afraid of you than of his father," said Takanatsu.

"Kaname never says anything to him. I wonder if it won't be harder for him to leave me than it would be to leave Kaname, though."

"When the divorce comes? But you'll be going out into the world stripped and alone, and his sympathies naturally will be with you."

"Do you really think so? . . . I think myself that most of the sympathy is going to collect around Kaname. On the surface at least it will be as though I am abandoning him, and people will blame me for it. I wonder if Hiroshi won't be bitter against me too when he starts hearing rumors."

"But later on he'll understand. Children retain a great deal, and when they grow up they start going over things and rejudging them from a grownup's point of view. This must have been this way, and that was that way, they say. That's why you have to be careful with children—some day they grow up."

Misako did not answer. She was still by the window, absently looking out. A small bird flitted from one branch to another of the plum trees. A thrush, she wondered. Or a lark? She followed it with her eye for a time. Beyond the plum trees Jiiya had the lid off a nursery frame and seemed to be transplanting shoots in the vegetable garden. The sea was not visible, but as she looked off into the clear sky over the harbor, she heaved an involuntary sigh.

"You don't have to go to Suma today?"

Misako laughed, shortly and a little bitterly, her head still averted.

"But you go almost every day now, don't you?"

"That's right."

"If you want to see him, why not go?"

"Am I so obviously the hussy?"

"I wonder if she wants to be told she is or she isn't."

"Tell me the truth."

"Well, we did agree yesterday that you had become a woman of the world and we could expect you to go even farther."

"I quite admit it—but, really, you needn't worry about today. I told him you would be here and I ought to stay at home—and it would hardly be polite to run off and leave you after all these presents."

"—she says. And yet she was away all day yesterday."

"But I thought Kaname would want to talk to you yesterday."

"And today is lady's day?"

"Anyway, let's go downstairs. I'm hungry. You can watch even if you don't want anything to eat."

"Which of these are you taking?"

"I haven't made up my mind. Leave your shop open and I'll look them over at my leisure. You may have had your breakfast, but I'm almost faint from hunger myself."

From the foot of the stairs they glanced into the

room below. Kaname had come in from the veranda and lay face-up on a sofa, still immersed in his book.

"Did you find anything good?" he asked mechanically as he heard them pass.

"It was most disappointing. He sends off elaborate notices on the presents he's bringing, and then when he gets here we find he's as closefisted as ever."

"Your wife is hopelessly greedy."

"But you said three of the cheap ones or two of the good ones."

"Please don't feel I'm forcing them on you. Think what I save if you don't take any at all."

Kaname laughed politely. They could hear him still flicking over the pages.

"It looks as though he'll be occupied for a while at least," said Takanatsu as they turned a corner to the Japanese wing.

"Almost anything can keep him occupied while it's new, but when the novelty wears off he'll have no more of it. He's like a child with a toy."

As they came into the breakfast room, Misako motioned Takanatsu to the cushion Kaname would normally have used at the head of the low sandalwood table, and took a place herself to one side.

"O-sayo, would you bring some toast, please?" She turned to the mulberry tea cabinet behind her. "Would you like black tea or green?"

"Either will do. And maybe you could offer me something sweet."

"How about a German pastry? I have some good ones from Juchheim's."

"Fine. I hate to sit and watch other people eat."

"Oh, dear, I thought I'd escaped, but I can smell something odd even here."

"Probably I've passed some of it on to you. Go to Suma tomorrow and see what Aso says."

" 'As long as you're seeing that individual Takanatsu, please stay away from me.' "

"But when two people are really in love, a slight smell of garlic makes no difference. If it does, they're only pretending."

"This with reference to your own successes? And what do I get for being your audience?"

"Aren't you quick with your conclusions! Possibly I do owe you something, though—how about a piece of toast?"

"I wonder if anyone ever really learned to like the smell of garlic."

"Indeed someone did. Yoshiko."

"It's not true, then, that she ran away because you smelled of garlic?"

"Kaname's invention. I'm told that even now she thinks of me when she smells garlic."

"And do you ever think of her?"

"I can't say I don't. But she's the sort of woman to go drinking with, not the sort to marry."

"A loose type?"

"Yes."

"Like me."

"Kaname says you really aren't at all. He thinks it's a surface you cultivate, and underneath you're a chaste wife and a virtuous mother."

"I wonder." Bending her full attention to the food before her, as though to cover a certain embarrassment, Misako put together a sandwich of sausage and chopped pickles and brought it delicately to her mouth.

"That looks good."

"It is good."

"And what are these little objects?"

"Liver sausages. From a German shop in Kobe."

"Your guest got nothing as fine for his breakfast."

"Of course not. This is reserved for my breakfast."

"I've concluded I would rather have that than a German pastry."

"What greed! Open your mouth and say 'Ah.'"

"Ah."

"That smell again. Be careful not to touch the fork, now. Take it delicately by the bread—that's right. How did you like it?"

"Delicious."

"I'll not give you any more. There will be none left for me."

"But you could have had O-sayo bring a fork for me too. Handing people things on your own fork—really, that is a little like a loose woman."

"If you have these objections, perhaps you should refrain from demanding other people's food."

"But you never used to have such bad manners. You used to be so quiet and ladylike."

"If I've changed, I've changed."

"Have you really changed, or are you only making a show?"

"Making a show?"

"Yes."

". . . I don't really know."

"Kaname says he's tried to change you. He says the responsibility is all his. I doubt if that's the whole truth."

"I'd as soon not have him taking the responsibility. It's only a hidden part of my nature finally coming out."

"I suppose there's always a little of the loose woman even in the most proper wife. But in your case aren't you pushed on by this difficulty with Kaname? You don't want people to see you as a lonely and unfortunate woman, and you deliberately try to seem gay."

"And that's what you call making a show?"

"I'm afraid you'd have to call it a sort of show. You don't want people to see that you're not loved by your husband—or am I saying more than I should?"

"It makes no difference. Please say exactly what comes to you."

"You try to be gay and lively to cover your weakness, but now and then the loneliness underneath shows through. Kaname sees it, I imagine, even if no one else does."

"But I'm so unnatural when he's around. Haven't you noticed a difference in me when I'm with him and when I'm not?"

"I'd say you seem less under control when you're away from him."

"You see? Even you have sensed it. Think how unpleasant it would be for him. And so I always find myself being very severe and proper in front of him. I simply can't help it."

"With Aso you're the loose woman? That side of you comes to the fore?"

"I'm sure it must."

"But once you're married again, you may be surprised at how that too changes."

"I don't think so, at least if it's Aso I'm married to."

"It's remarkable, though, how often women do change

69

after they're married. Right now you're playing a game."

"And it's not possible for marriage to be a game?"

"It's splendid if it can be."

"I intend mine to be. I think people take marriage much too seriously."

"And then when you're tired of him you get another divorce?"

"That's a reasonable conclusion, I suppose."

"I'm not talking about reasonable conclusions. I'm talking about your own intentions."

Misako's fork, on the point of taking up a pickle, stopped dead in her plate.

"The time will come when you'll be tired of him?"

"I don't intend it to."

"And Aso?"

"I don't think he expects to be tired of me either, but he says it wouldn't help to have to make promises."

"And is that enough for you?"

"I understand well enough how he feels. He could promise never to get tired of me. But this is the first time he's been in love, and no matter what his intentions are, he can't know how his feelings might change. No matter how much he may intend now never to change, he can't really be sure what will happen. He says it would be meaningless to promise something he can't be sure of, and he says he doesn't like telling lies."

"But that's quite the wrong attitude. If he's not in love seriously enough to go ahead and promise without a thought for the future . . ."

"Doesn't it depend on the individual, though? He's always analyzing himself, and it's simply not possible for him to make a promise with reservations, no matter how serious he might be."

"I think I would go ahead and make the promise even if there was a chance it might turn out to be a lie."

"But with Aso it's different. If he were to make a rash promise it would have exactly the wrong effect. 'Am I getting tired of her?' it would make him say. That's what he's afraid of—he knows how he is. It would be much better not to make any promises, to get married in the mood we've been in all along. He says the marriage will have much more chance of lasting if he can go into it without tying his feelings up in promises."

"He may be right, but it's somehow a little too—"

"Yes?"

"A little too much like a game."

"I feel much more secure when I know he's being frank. I understand him."

"Have you mentioned this to Kaname?"

"I haven't had a chance to. And, besides, it would do no good."

"But you're being much too reckless. Leaving your husband when you have no real guarantee for your future." Takanatsu, trying to control a rising sharpness in his tone, stopped for a moment as he noticed that Misako was blinking rapidly, her hands folded tightly in her lap. "I certainly hadn't thought it was as bad as all this. . . . I shouldn't say so, I know, but I'd have expected you to be calmer, more sober. After all, you're discarding a husband."

"But I am being sober. . . . It's only that, either way, I have to get out of this house."

"And so you should have thought everything over more carefully before you let yourself come to this impasse."

"What good would it have done? You don't know how hard it is for me to stay on here now that we're not really married. . . ."

Misako's shoulders were straight and her head was bowed. She tried hard to hold back her tears, but a shiny drop fell to her knee.

# CHAPTER EIGHT

KANAME had abandoned himself to a search for the passages that have given *The Arabian Nights* its dubious reputation. Even this first volume, which went only from the first to the thirty-fourth nights, contained three hundred and sixty octavo pages, however, and to comb through the whole seventeen would be a formidable task. Sometimes he stopped at an engaging illustration, but the text beside it generally turned out to be quite ordinary. The table of contents—"Tale of the Wazir and the Sage

Duban," "Tale of the Three Apples," "The Nazarene Broker's Story," "Tale of the Ensorcelled Prince"—was little help. He began reading over the notes (there were careful notes on almost every page of this Burton Club edition, the first complete translation). Many of them were concerned with linguistic problems of little interest to Kaname, but among them he found some that described intriguing Arab customs or suggested something about the contents of the text proper.

*"A large hollow navel is looked upon not only as a beauty, but in children it is held a promise of good growth. . . .*

*"A slight parting between the two front incisors, the upper only, is considered a beauty by Arabs; why it is hard to say except for the racial love of variety. . . .*

*"The King's barber is usually a man of rank for the best of reasons that he holds his Sovereign's life between his fingers. One of these noble Figaros in India married an English lady who was, they say, unpleasantly surprised to find out what were her husband's official duties. . . .*

*"In the Moslem East a young woman, single or married, is not allowed to appear alone in the streets; and the police has a right to arrest delinquents. As a preventive of intrigues the precaution is excellent. During the Crimean war hundreds of officers, English, French and Italian, became familiar with Constantinople; and not a few flattered themselves on their success with Turkish women. I do not believe that a single bonâ fide case occurred; the 'conquests' were all Greeks, Wallachians, Armenians, or Jews. . . .*

*"Lane (i, 124) is scandalized and naturally enough by this scene, which is the only blot in an admirable tale admirably told. . . ."*

Kaname drew up short—here it was, finally—and quickly reread the last footnote. "Lane (i, 124) is scandalized . . . admirable tale admirably told. Yet even here the grossness is but little more pronounced than what we find in our old drama (e.g., Shakespeare's *King Henry V*) written for the stage, whereas tales like The Nights are not read or recited before both sexes."

He turned immediately to the beginning of "The Porter and the Three Ladies of Bagdad," the tale thus annotated. He had gone no farther than the first five or six lines when he heard steps from the direction of the Japanese wing and Takanatsu came in.

"Can't you put that away for a few minutes?"

"What's the trouble?" Kaname made no motion toward getting up from the sofa, but, reluctant though he was to leave off reading for even a moment, he did lay the volume face-down on his leg.

"I've just heard something very odd."

"And what have you heard that's very odd?"

Takanatsu walked silently up and down beside the table for a time, his cigar trailing a line of smoke off behind him like a mist.

"I've actually been told that Misako has no guarantees for her future."

"No guarantees for her future?"

"You're sometimes careless yourself, but Misako is really much too careless."

"What are you talking about? Please don't go throwing thunderbolts about with no explanation."

"Misako and Aso have made no promise to go on loving each other. Aso says he can't promise because love has a way of wearing off and there's no way of being sure what might happen. Misako seems to have agreed."

"That's the sort of thing he'd say." Kaname, finally resigned to being interrupted, folded over the page, closed the book, and pulled himself up from the sofa.

"I don't know him myself of course and I'm in no position to attack him, but I don't approve of his argument. It could seem fairly vicious, depending on how you chose to look at it."

"But does a decent man make promises just to please a woman? Isn't it more honest to refuse to?"

"I don't like that sort of honesty. It's not honesty, it's lack of steadiness."

"You have your nature, others have theirs. No matter how well matched two people seem to be, the time comes when they get tired of each other, and there's a great deal of merit in saying that you can't make promises about the future. If I were Aso, I think I should do very much the same thing."

73

"And when they do get tired of each other they separate?"

"Getting tired of each other and separating are different matters. When the first love begins to fade, a sort of domestic affection takes its place. Isn't that what most marriages are built on, as a matter of fact?"

"That's very well if this Aso is dependable, but what if he should say he's sick of her and throw her away? Isn't it a little disturbing to think that there are no guarantees against it?"

"I don't think he's likely to do that."

"I suppose you had a private detective after him before you let things go this far?"

"I did not."

"You had some other way of investigating, then?"

"I didn't really do anything in particular. . . . I don't like the idea of spying, and it's such a nuisance."

"You're impossible." Takanatsu almost spat out the words. "When you said he was such a fine, upstanding individual, I assumed you had investigated him. This is really too irresponsible. How do you know he's not a sex fiend or a swindler out after Misako? What would you do if he should turn out to be?"

"When you put it that way, it does worry me a little. . . . But when I met him he seemed a very high type, not the sort you suggest at all. Actually, though, I put my faith more in Misako. She's no child, and she can surely tell the difference between a decent man and a scoundrel. If Misako is sure of him, that's enough to satisfy me."

"But that's exactly what you can least count on. Women may seem clever enough, but they're fools."

"I'd rather you wouldn't talk that way. I've tried to keep my mind off the worst possibilities."

"And let everything take its course. You are a strange one. It's exactly because you leave problems like this unsettled that you haven't been able to work yourself into a decision on the divorce itself."

"I suppose I should have investigated earlier. But it can't do any good now." Kaname spoke as if it were no problem of his and fell listlessly over on the sofa again.

He had no idea what sort of feelings Misako and Aso had for each other. To try to imagine the nature of his wife's love affair is hardly pleasant for even the coldest husband, and while Kaname did sometimes feel a certain curiosity, he always hurried to push disturbing speculations from his mind.

The affair between Misako and Aso dated from some two years before. Kaname came back from the city one day to find Misako on the veranda talking to a strange man. "Mr. Aso," she said shortly. Since they had in the course of time come to build up their own independent friendships, Kaname did not find any further explanation necessary. He gathered that Misako and Aso had become acquainted at a school in Kobe where Misako had taken up French as a cure for boredom. That was all he knew at the time. Misako began to be more careful of her appearance, but Kaname quite overlooked the assortment of cosmetics and toilet articles steadily building up on her dresser—testimony indeed to the apathy into which he had fallen as a husband. It was nearly a year before he finally noticed the change.

One night as she lay in bed with the covers pulled up to her forehead, he heard her sobbing quietly; long into the night he lay staring into the darkness of the room, listening. It was not the first time he had been assailed by this sobbing in the night. A year or two after they were married, when he was beginning to withdraw from her sexually, he had often enough had to meet the same accusing evidence of the woman's wretchedness. He knew what it meant and he felt intensely sorry for her. At the same time he was conscious of being pushed farther from her; and, at a loss for a way to console her, he let the sobbing pass in silence. Would he have to spend the rest of his life with it, who knew how many years?—the prospect made him long to be alone and free. Gradually she seemed to accept her loneliness, however, and the sobbing stopped.

And now, after years of respite, it had started again. Kaname at first doubted his ears, then asked himself how to account for this extraordinary development. Why should she have started again? What case could she be pleading now? Had she never resigned herself at all, only waited for the day when his affection for her would return, and now, after years of waiting, had she found it impossible to wait any longer? What a fool the woman was, he thought; and, as years before, he let the tears pass in silence. But night after night they continued. Quite unable to find an explanation, he finally told her she was making a nuisance of herself.

At that Misako broke into open and unrestrained sobbing. "Forgive me. There's something I've kept from you," she said softly, her voice choked with tears.

Kaname could not have denied that he was a little shocked at the words, but more than that he felt as though the shackles had opened, as though a heavy weight had suddenly and unexpectedly been lifted from his shoulders. He could go out into the wide fields again and breathe freely of the clean air—and as if to prove it, he took in a long breath to the bottom of his lungs as he lay there face-up in bed.

Misako said that the affair had gone no farther than a declaration of affection, and he saw no reason to doubt her. Even so, her confession seemed enough to cancel out the debt he had been carrying. Had he in fact turned her, pushed her to another man, he wondered—if he had, then he could only be revolted at his own baseness. But in all honesty he had simply held a secret hope that something like this might happen. He had never told her of it, and so far as he could remember he had never created incidents that might bring about her fall. In an excess of pain at being unable to love her as a husband should, he had only nursed a prayer, almost a dream, that someone might come along to give the luckless woman what he himself could not. But Misako's character being what it was, he had never thought the prospects very good.

"And have you found someone too?" she asked after she had told him of Aso. It was clear that she had nursed a hope not too different from his.

He answered that he had not. Perhaps the really unforgivable thing was that he had forced her to remain continent while he had not been at pains to remain so himself. He had found no one, he said; but he had in fact let his curiosity and his physical appetites drive him— indeed, only for a moment now and then—to the company of certain unwholesome women. For Kaname a woman had to be either a goddess or a plaything. Possibly the real reason for his failure with Misako was that she could be neither. Had she not been his wife he

76

might have been able to look on her as a plaything, and the fact that she was his wife made it impossible for him to find her interesting.

"I've kept this much respect for you, I think," he said later that same night. "I may not have been able to love you, but I've been careful not to use you for my own pleasure."

At that Misako broke into violent sobbing. "I understand that—I'm even almost grateful for it. But I've wanted to be loved more than I have been, even if it meant being used."

Even after Misako's confession, Kaname made no effort to urge her into Aso's arms. He said only enough to show that he claimed no right to pronounce her love affair improper and that he could not object, whatever it might develop into. And yet almost certainly his very refusal to call it improper had the indirect effect of sending her on to Aso. What she wanted from him was not this understanding, this sympathy, this generosity. "I don't know myself what to do. I'm terribly mixed up," she said. "If you tell me I should, I can still back out." She would probably have been overjoyed had he said imperiously: "This foolishness must stop." And even had he called her affair not illicit but only unwise, she would probably still have been able to leave Aso. That was what she wanted. Deep in her heart she no longer hoped for any love from the husband who had withdrawn so from her; but she did hope that he would somehow bring this new love of hers under control, put an end to it. When she asked what to do, however, he only sighed and said: "I have no idea." Aso's visits became more frequent and Misako took to going out oftener and to staying out later at night, and Kaname never attempted to interfere or indicated any displeasure by so much as a frown. She would have to dispose of this new passion, the first in her life, by means of her own.

Even afterwards he sometimes heard her sobbing in the night, no doubt from an excess of wretchedness at being turned away by this stone of a husband and yet unable to throw herself decisively into the world of her new love. Especially on nights after she had had a letter from Aso or had met him somewhere, Kaname would hear her quiet sobbing, muffled by the bedclothes, through

77

to the dawn. One morning, perhaps half a year later, he
called her into the western wing. "I've something to talk
to you about," he said. There were early daffodils on
the table, he remembered, and the electric stove was
going. It must have been a bright, clear winter morning.
They faced each other swollen-eyed across the table—
she had cried until daybreak again the night before and
he himself had not been able to sleep. He had thought
of talking to her during the night, but there was a possibility that Hiroshi might wake up, and there was a
possibility too that Misako, always ready with tears
even in the daytime, might become still more emotional
in the dark. He decided that the fresh morning hours
would be better.

"There's something I've been thinking for a long time
I'd like to talk over," he said, trying to sound light and
pleasant, as though perhaps he were inviting her out for
a picnic.

"And there's something I've been wanting to talk
over," Misako parroted back as she pulled her chair up
near the stove. There was a suggestion of a smile in the
corners of her eyes, red though they were from lack of
sleep.

It presently became clear that the two of them had
reached very much the same conclusions by the same
route. Kaname said that it was impossible for them to
love each other now, and that, though they might with
their recognition of each other's good points and their
knowledge of each other's weaknesses find themselves
happily mated ten, twenty years hence, on the edge of
old age, there was no point in relying on anything as
indefinite as that; and Misako said she agreed. They had
both concluded too that, while they were held together
by affection for Hiroshi, it would be foolish to make
fossils of themselves for no better reason than that. But
when Kaname asked: "Would you like to separate, then?"
Misako answered: "Would you?" They knew that divorce was the solution, and yet neither had the courage
to propose it, each was left face to face with his own
weakness.

Kaname had no real cause to throw his wife out. He
would only feel worse once the separation was over if the
initiative had been his, and he wanted to be the passive

partner. Since Misako had someone to marry and he had no one, he hoped that she would make the decision. But for Misako the fact that she had a lover and Kaname had none, that she alone of the two would be happy, only made it the more difficult to take the first step. True, she was not loved by her husband. She could not say, though, that she had been cruelly mistreated. If one was always looking for something better, then of course there was no end to one's demands; but the world was full of unfortunate wives, and Misako, unloved but with little else to complain of, could not find it in her to make that alone the reason for abandoning her husband and child. In a word, both husband and wife wanted to be discarded; each hoped to put himself in a position where that would happen. But why, since they were presumably adults, did they find themselves so paralyzed at the task before them? Why were they so afraid to do what reason told them must be done? Was it simply that they were incapable of turning away from the past? Others had evidently found that time softened the pain (though certainly there was pain), once a separation was complete.

"With us I suppose it's that we're more afraid of what's in front of our noses than of what's still a distance off," Kaname said with a laugh.

At the end of the conversation Kaname came to his proposal. "We'll have to arrange," he said by way of preface, "so that we'll be drifting into a divorce and hardly knowing it."

The ancients would perhaps have called it girlish sentimentality, this inability to face up squarely to the sorrow of a farewell. Nowadays, however, one is counted clever if one can reach a goal without tasting the sorrow, however slight it may be, that seems to lie along the way. Kaname and Misako were cowardly, and there was no point in being ashamed of it. They could only accommodate themselves to their cowardice and follow its peculiar way to happiness.

Kaname recited the set of principles he had been carrying nicely composed in his mind:

"1. To satisfy appearances, Misako is for the present to remain Kaname's wife.

79

"2. Similarly for the sake of appearances, Aso is to be for the present a friend only.

"3. To the extent that it will not arouse suspicion, Misako's love for Aso, both physical and spiritual, is to be given free license.

"4. If after a period of two or three years it appears that Misako and Aso are affectionate and compatible and are in prospect of being happily married, Kaname will take principal responsibility for gaining the consent of Misako's family, and will formally relinquish her to Aso.

"5. This period of two or three years is therefore to be considered a testing of the affections of Misako and Aso for each other. If it appears that the test has failed, and that the two, because of incompatibilities which have emerged, could not make a successful marriage, Misako will remain in Kaname's house as she has to now.

"6. If, happily, the experiment is a success, Kaname will continue to regard the two as friends after they are married."

As Kaname finished speaking, he saw Misako's face light up bright as this winter morning. "Thank you," she said simply. There were happy tears in her eyes, as though for the first time in years the turmoil in her heart had quieted, as though she could finally look up untroubled into the open sky. Kaname, as he watched her, felt that his chains too had snapped. In all the years they had been together they had been tormented by an irritant like a fragment lodged between two back teeth. Now, ironically, they felt it dissolve, they felt a coming together without restraint, when for the first time they spoke openly of separation.

It was of course a bold adventure, but unless they closed their eyes and let themselves fall step by step into a position from which there would be no withdrawing, the divorce probably would never come. It was not likely that Aso would object. Indeed, Kaname took special pains, when he explained the proposal, to point out its risks. "There are probably countries in the West where no one would raise an eyebrow at this sort of thing. But Japan hasn't yet come that far, and if we are to carry it off I'm afraid we're going to have to be extremely careful. The most important thing of course is for us to trust each other. And no matter what good intentions we may have, it will be easy enough to make mistakes. We shall all of us be in a difficult position, and we shall have to be careful not to hurt any feelings and not to cause any unnecessary embarrassment. You will keep all of this in mind, I'm sure."

After that Aso's visits stopped and Misako began "going to Suma."

Kaname closed his eyes to the affair. If only he relaxed, his fate would take care of itself—thus he gave himself up to the current and made no effort of the will other than that required to cling, blindly and with singleness of purpose, to the direction in which it seemed to be taking him. But the end of the experiment, the day when a decision would have to be made, loomed ever more fearsome. No matter how he tried to glide along, there was still the moment of parting to be faced. It could not be avoided. He felt as though, on a course that had seemed calm and smooth, a typhoon belt had appeared and was somehow to be got through. He had kept his eyes carefully shut, but they would one day have to open. The prevision of it made him the more prone to seek yet a moment's refuge in the comfortable drift.

"On the one hand you say it's hard to leave her, and on the other you pamper yourself with this wild unsteadiness. I couldn't tolerate it myself," Takanatsu said.

"My unsteadiness is nothing new. Anyway, it seems to me that ethics have to be modified a little to suit the individual. Everyone has to build his own scheme and try to apply it."

"True, I suppose. And in your scheme unsteadiness is a virtue?"

"I don't say it's exactly a virtue, but I do say it's wrong for someone who was born indecisive to go against his nature and force himself into decisions. If he does, he generally adds to his losses and in the end he is worse off than ever. Indecisive people have to choose a course that suits them. To take my case: the final goal is a divorce, and if I reach that goal eventually, it doesn't matter how many evasions and detours I go through on the way. I don't think it would matter if I were even more unsteady—as you call it—than I am."

"I suspect from the way you talk that it will take a lifetime for you to get through to your goal."

"I've honestly thought so too. They say that in the West adultery is a common thing, at least among the upper classes. Most often it's not the kind where the husband and wife are deceiving each other, but the kind where each one recognizes and ignores it—very much like my own case. I often think that if society in this country would only allow it, I could be content with some such arrangement as that for the rest of my life."

"It's out of style even in the West. Marriages aren't held together any more by religion."

"But it's not only a question of religion. I wonder if even foreigners aren't afraid to cut the old ties too quickly."

"Well, I shall leave you to do as you like. I'm through." Takanatsu brusquely took up the volume of *The Arabian Nights,* which had slipped to the floor.

"Why do you say that?"

"You should know. It's not for an outsider to get himself involved in a problem as cloudy as yours."

"But it will be harder if you don't help."

"Let it be harder, then. I've nothing to suggest."

"Whether you have or you haven't, it will be hard for us if you run away. It will only make things cloudier still. Really, I beg of you."

"Well, tonight I'll take Hiroshi to Tokyo with me." There was little encouragement in Takanatsu's voice as he leafed coldly through the book.

## CHAPTER NINE

"I WOULD *join the song-thrush*
  *And sing my way up the river*
  *To meet spring in Miyako.*"

Her samisen tuned to the proper low mode, O-hisa was singing an old Osaka song. The Osaka folksong can be coarse and crude, but this particular one the old man

liked. It had in it a touch of Tokyo verve that perhaps
appealed to him, son of Tokyo that he was, even now
that he had "surrendered" to Osaka. Then too, as he
pointed out, the samisen refrain that broke into the
lyrics seemed ordinary enough at first, but if one listened for it one could find deep down the sound of the
River Yodo.

*"Held back by the winter wind,*
  *By the clinging willow branches,*
  *I walk, untrained to walk—*
  *How many times now,*
  *Up and back?—*
  *This strand to Hachikenya.*
  *Pressed close together all the night*
  *We lie. What is it wakes us?*
  *The crows at Amijima?*
  *The bells at Kanzanji?"*

Through the open second-floor window they could see
the harbor in the gathering dusk, separated from them
by only the waterfront road. A straits ferry, one would
guess from its name, was preparing to put out to sea. It
was a tiny ship, of no more than four or five hundred
tons, and yet its stern almost brushed against the dock
as its prow came round, so narrow was the harbor. Kaname sat on the veranda and looked out at the concrete
breakwater, small and dainty as a piece of rock candy.
At the end of it was an equally diminutive lighthouse, its
light already burning even though the sea was still a
pale evening gold. Two or three men were fishing at its
base. The scene was hardly striking, but it had about it a
certain air of the south that one does not find in the provinces around Tokyo. Kaname thought of how, twenty
years before, it must have been, he had once visited a
small town on the coast north of Tokyo. There had been
a light on each of the two points at the harbor mouth,
and the little harbor, its waterfront lined with pleasure
houses, had struck him as in its way the very model
of the old boatman's town. But in contrast with the decay of the one in the north, this southern harbor was
gay, warm, full of the joy of life. Like most natives of
Tokyo, Kaname rather tended to stay at home, and here

on the veranda, cooling himself in a cotton summer kimono, it struck him as somewhat laughable that a trip across an arm of the Inland Sea to an island almost in Kobe harbor should seem a major expedition. He had not been especially enthusiastic when the old man had asked him to come along on this visit to the thirty-three holy places of Awaji. He foresaw that he would not find it soothing to have to watch the old man and O-hisa together, and in any case it seemed best not to risk making a nuisance of himself.

"Come, now. There's no need to be so bashful," the old man said. "I want to stay a couple of days in the harbor first and see the Awaji puppet theater—it's supposed to be the ancestor of the one in Osaka, you know. After that we'll dress ourselves up like pilgrims and do the holy places. Why don't you come along at least as far as the harbor?"

O-hisa added her persuasions, and Kaname, with the impression of the Osaka puppets strong in his mind, had to admit that he did feel some curiosity about the Awaji theater.

"Maybe you should get yourself up to look like a pilgrim too, since you're so intrigued with the idea," Misako said with a frown.

When he thought of the fragile O-hisa made over into a winsome pilgrim of the Kabuki and of the old man at her side ringing a pilgrim's bell and intoning a canticle from one holy place to the next, Kaname could not help being a little envious. The old man chose his pleasures well. Kaname had heard that it was not uncommon for men of taste in Osaka to dress a favorite geisha as a pilgrim and do the Awaji circuit with her every year. The old man, much taken with the idea, announced that he would make this the first of an annual series. Always afraid of sunburn, O-hisa was less enthusiastic.

"How does it go? We sleep at Hachikenya, is it? Where do you suppose Hachikenya is?" Kaname asked.

As O-hisa laid down the polished horn plectrum, the old man touched his finger to the silver flask he was heating unhurriedly over charcoal. The favored red-lacquer cups were ready in front of him. Even though it was a warm May day, he had thrown a dark-blue cloak over his cotton kimono. "You're from Tokyo, of course, and you wouldn't know." He took the flask from the charcoal. "The Osaka barges used to start up the River Yodo for Kyoto from the Temma Bridge, and the boathouses were just above at Hachikenya."

"I see. So we're sleeping at Hachikenya. And Amijima is on the river just above that, which would explain the crows."

"Right. The best thing about this song is that it's short. Most of the Osaka songs are so long they put you to sleep. This one is just the right length to keep you interested."

"How about another one, O-hisa?"

"No, she's incompetent. When young women sing this sort of song they make it too pretty. The samisen should be coarser, I tell her, but she won't understand. She goes through it as though it were a concert piece."

"If you find it so unpleasant," said O-hisa, "perhaps you should play something yourself."

"No, no. Go ahead. We'll have another from you."

"I don't really know why I should." Pouting like a spoiled child, O-hisa took up the samisen to retune it.

O-hisa was called upon to pamper the demanding old man to a really extraordinary degree. He for his part lavished affection on her as on his principal treasure. He trained her in the arts, in cooking, in dress, wherever it was possible to cultivate and refine her, so that when he died she would have no trouble making a new match as she wished. It was doubtful in the final analysis, however, whether the regimen was appropriate for the modern young woman. O-hisa was allowed to see only puppet shows and to eat only insubstantial Japanese delicacies, and it was hard to believe that she was really satisfied with no more. Now and then she must want to see a movie or to eat a beefsteak. Kaname could admire her forbearance, which he credited to the fact that she had been reared in Kyoto, but at the same time he found it hard to understand the workings of a spirit so submissive. The old man had once been intent on having her master the rough tearoom style of flower arranging. That field of interest had now given way to the old folksong. Once a week the two of them made their way to the southern outskirts of Osaka to take lessons from a blind musician. The old man's whims were to be seen here too, in the fact that they purposely went to Osaka when there were

85

certainly teachers enough to choose from in Kyoto. It may have been that he had found his evidence in the seventeenth-century beauties on a Matahei screen, but he insisted that the samisen for the folksong was best held not on the knee but at the side in the Osaka fashion. There was great charm in the figure of a young girl seated on a cushion, he said, with her body slightly twisted to hold the Osaka samisen. It was hopeless to look for O-hisa to master the instrument at her age, and one would do better to attend to the way she held herself. His pleasure really came more from watching her than from listening to her.

"Don't be cross, now. Let's have another," said Kaname.

"What would you like?"

"Anything. Something I know if that seems possible."

"How about 'Snow'?" The old man poured Kaname a cup of saké. "Kaname's probably heard that."

" 'Snow' and 'Dark Hair' are almost the only ones I do know."

As Kaname listened to the music, a memory came back from his childhood. Before the earthquake, the merchants' houses in the Kuramae district of downtown Tokyo, where he grew up, had latticed fronts, rather like those in the Nishijin craftsmen's section of Kyoto now, so narrow that the houses looked smaller from the outside than they actually were. Room followed room in a straggling line back from the lattice, until one came to a tiny court and garden, and over a corridor skirting it to a fairly large detached wing at the very back where the family living-rooms were. The houses to the left and right were built on the same plan, so that when one looked out from the second floor, one could see a garden and a veranda beyond spike-topped fences on either side. . . . The old merchants' quarter, when he thought back on it, was wonderfully quiet for all that the neighbors were so close. Memory had of course been blurred by the years, but it seemed to him that he had never heard a sound from either of the two neighboring houses. It was as though no one lived beyond those fences, so quiet was it, so completely undisturbed by human voices—as though one had ventured into an old samurai villa in a dying provincial castle town.

And yet now and then, he hardly knew when, there

86

had been the low echo of a girl's voice singing to a koto. It belonged to one Fu-chan, he heard. Fu-chan was reputed to be a very pretty girl, but he had never seen her and had no particular desire to meet her. One day, however—it must have been an evening in summer—he was looking out from an upstairs window and saw turned toward him the faint, white face of a girl who had taken a cushion out to the veranda and sat with her back against the open summer doors, looking up at the evening sky and the mosquitoes in their column-like swarms. His young heart ravished at the sight, he pulled back from the window almost as though he had taken fright at something, so quickly that he retained no clear impression of her features. The attraction was perhaps too slight a one to be called a first love. Still, it dominated his childhood thoughts and dreams for some time after, and it was probably the first sprouting of that woman-worship Takanatsu noted.

Even now he had no idea how old the girl had been. To a boy of seven or eight, fourteen or fifteen and twenty alike look grown up, and as her slender figure gave an impression of maturity, she seemed all the more his senior. He remembered uncertainly that there was an ashtray at her knee and that she held a long pipe in her hand; but there was in those days still something left in the manner of the women of downtown Tokyo that suggested the bold urbanity of the last years before Japan was opened to the West—his mother, for instance, liked to tuck up the sleeves of her kimono in warm weather—and the fact that the girl smoked was not real evidence that she was grown up.

Kaname's family moved away from Kuramae perhaps four to five years later, leaving him with only that one glimpse over the fence at Fu-chan. He found himself listening afterwards to the koto and the songs it accompanied. His mother told him that one song the girl seemed especially to like was called "Snow." It was composed originally for the koto, she explained, but it was sometimes sung to the samisen, and in Tokyo it was known as "an Osaka song." Kaname did not hear it again after they left Kuramae, and it lay in his mind dormant and as well as forgotten until ten years or more later when he was on a pleasure trip to Kyoto and was watching a little Gion dancer in a teahouse. One of her dances, he recognized with an indescribably poignant surge of memory, was to the accompaniment of this same "Snow." An old geisha, of perhaps fifty, was singing, her voice heavy with the sad mellowness of age, and the Kyoto samisen had a muffled, languid tone, a sort of low tolling quality—Kaname thought he knew what the old man meant when he demanded more "coarseness." O-hisa's singing was indeed too pretty, too lacking in this throaty suggestiveness. But Fu-chan those years before had had the same bell-like voice as O-hisa. The latter's singing was therefore a still more powerful inciter of memories, and her samisen, tuned in the Osaka style, called up the sound of the koto more effectively than the low, dull Kyoto samisen could.

O-hisa's samisen was made so that the neck could be detached, dismembered, and put inside the body. When they went on outings the old man always took it along and forced the reluctant O-hisa to play for him. This happened at hotels and inns, and if the spirit moved him he was as likely as not to take out the samisen in a busy roadside teahouse or under a blossoming cherry tree. They had floated singing down the River Uji under the October full moon the year before, and it was the old man who had caught the severe cold.

"Now it's your turn." O-hisa pushed the samisen toward the old man.

"Did you understand the words, Kaname?" He took up the samisen with a show of indifference and began tuning it to a lower key, but he was not quite able to hide his pleasure at having an audience. Possibly because he had had some training in Kyoto music before he left Tokyo, he was not without skill at Osaka folksongs, late though he had come to them. The amateur listening to him found a certain charm and polish in his style. Vastly proud of himself, he made the way difficult for O-hisa by scolding her as a famous teacher might.

"I have the feeling that I understand vaguely, but I'd probably come up with something wild if I tried to go at it grammatically."

"Quite true. . . . The composers didn't think about grammar. If you see generally what was in their hearts, that's really enough. The vagueness is rich in its own way. Take this for example." He began singing:

*"Stagnant as this marsh,*
 *As the waters of this Nozawa,*
 *Still my heart lights up,*
 *If for a moment only,*
 *At the moon that steals through my window.*

" 'While we move in the wide world,' it goes on from there . . . but that first part is about a man who visits a woman secretly at night. Instead of anything direct we have the moon stealing in through the window. And isn't it better really to leave things only hinted at? O-hisa sings it without thinking what it means. That's why she misses the spirit of it."

"I suppose it could mean that, now that you explain it. But I doubt if many people guess—even people who think they know the song."

"The real charm of these songs is that the composers didn't really care whether most people understood or not. It was enough if a few bothered to puzzle out the meaning. Most of the songs were composed by blind men, after all, and they have a sort of dark, twisted quality themselves."

The old man had to be a little drunk before he would sing. Having reached the proper stage, he screwed his eyes shut and threw himself into the music as though he were a blind minstrel himself.

Like most people his age, he was in the habit of going to bed early and getting up early. At eight he was in bed with O-hisa beside him massaging his shoulders. Kaname withdrew to his room across the hall, the influence of the saké still heavy on him. He thought of forcing himself to sleep early, but he was trained to late hours. Although he dozed off now and then, he was not able really to get to sleep. There had been a time when he would have considered it a rare privilege to sleep alone. Kept awake night after night by Misako's sobbing, he used to go away sometimes to a resort near Tokyo where he could rest undisturbed and make up for the nights of wakefulness. Now that he and Misako no longer figured very large in each other's lives, however, it had become possible for him to sleep quite happily beside her, and, indeed, left with a bedroom to himself now for the first time in a great many days, he found that the muffled voices of the old man and O-hisa across the hall disturbed him more than Misako would have. The old man seemed to soften as though into a different person, even the timbre of his voice changed, when he was alone with O-hisa. Apparently they guessed that Kaname would be listening. Their sleepy voices, hushed as though to keep a secret, were no more than an affectionate murmur—he might have been less on edge had he been able to make out what they were saying. A low, steady pulsing beat along the floor to his pillow as the massaging went patiently on.

Still the old man talked. O-hisa answered chiefly in monosyllables, interjecting only now and then a sentence at the end of which Kaname could catch a Kyoto lilt. Though he felt a certain envy when he saw a happily married couple and drew a comparison with himself and Misako, still he was generally conscious of a vicarious pleasure mixed in with it. But this couple with thirty years' difference in their ages did upset him, prepared though he should have been for what he found. He thought how much more upset he would be if the old man were his father, and he thought he understood the strong dislike Misako had for O-hisa.

The old man seemed to have fallen asleep. Kaname could hear his low, steady breathing, and the soft pulsing as the steadfast O-hisa went on with the massage. It must have been nearly ten when she stopped. Kaname snapped on the light in his room as the light went out in the other. With no better amusement in prospect, he began writing postcards in bed, a picture postcard to Hiroshi with a quick note, and one to Takanatsu in Shanghai with seven or eight lines cramped in beside a view of the straits.

*How have you been? We have got nowhere since you abandoned us, and things are as cloudy as ever. Misako continues to go to Suma. I am here at Awaji with her father, where I am being treated to a demonstration of domestic affection. Misako dislikes O-hisa, but I have to admire her devotion even while I am being made uncomfortable by it.*

*I shall let you know when we have a solution though it is quite impossible to say now when that is likely to be.*

# CHAPTER TEN

"GOOD morning," Kaname called in from the hall. "May I come in?"

"Please. We're quite presentable."

He went into their room, which looked out to the front of the inn, and found O-hisa seated before the mirror at work on the upswept rolls of her Japanese coiffure. She was dressed in a cotton kimono tied at the waist with a narrow checkered sash. The old man, beside her, was on the point of taking out his thick glasses to study a leaflet that lay on his knee. The sea, clear into the distance, was so bright a blue that it turned black as one stared at it. Even the smoke from the ships seemed motionless. Now and then, with the faintest breath of a breeze, the leaflet stirred very slightly and a tear in the paper door rustled like a kite.

*AWAJI GENNOJÓ THEATER*
*Licensed by the Ministry of the Interior*
*Tokiwabridge, Sumoto*
*Program for the Third Day*

*Morning-Glory Diary*
    *Firefly Hunt on the River Uji*
    *Farewell at Akashi*
    *Yuminosuke's Villa*
    *Teahouse at Óiso*
    *Mount Maya*
    *Shelter at Hamamatsu*
    *Tokuemon's Inn*
    *Along the Way*

*Extra*
    The Tenth Scene from *Taikōki*
    *The Love of Oshun and Dembei*

*Guest Performance*
          *Stammering Matahei*
          (recited by Toyotake Rodayū
          of the Osaka Bunraku Theater)

*Admission:*
          50 sen
          30 sen for those entitled to discount

"Do you know of a scene in a teahouse at Ōiso?" the old man asked O-hisa.

"What play is it in?"

*"Morning-Glory Diary."*

"Teahouse at Ōiso. . . . I wonder if there is such a scene."

"So you see they put in scenes that are hardly ever played in Osaka. . . . Next comes Mount Maya. What would that be?"

"Wouldn't it be the one where Miyuki is kidnapped?"

"You're probably right. . . . She's kidnapped and taken to Hamamatsu. But in that case what happens to the moor at Makuzu? Isn't there supposed to be a scene on the moor at Makuzu?"

O-hisa had a comb in her mouth and did not answer. The fingers of her right hand were pressed lightly to one of her rolls of hair. A hand mirror she held behind her to reflect into the dresser sent the sun dancing brightly around the room.

Kaname still had no real idea how old she was. It suited the old man's tastes to search the old-clothes shops at Gojō and the morning bazaars at Kitano for materials no longer in style, for crepes and brocades tightly woven in small, subdued patterns, heavy and stiff as strands of chain. O-hisa was forced into them, protesting helplessly at "the musty old tatters." The somberness of her dress made her look to be in her late twenties—and indeed it appeared that she had been instructed by the old man to say she was, so that they might seem a slightly better-matched couple—but the glow of her pink fingers, their fine pattern of ridges cleanly marked as she held the mirror in her left hand, was not simply a product of the oil in her hair, Kaname felt sure. He had never seen her so informally dressed before. The flesh of her shoulders and thighs, swelling through the thin kimono, seemed with its richness to deny her pretensions as a delicate, refined Kyoto maiden, and told clearly that she could be no more than twenty-two or twenty-three at the most.

"Then the inn," the old man continued, "and the last scene on the road."

"I see."

"The first I've heard of a travel scene in *Morning-Glory Diary*," put in Kaname. "Miyuki has finally found Komazawa and they're going off together?"

"No, I've seen it. They leave the inn, you remember, and Miyuki is stopped at the ford after Komazawa has crossed? Well, in the last scene she's got across and is hurrying down Tōkaidō Highway after him."

"She's alone?"

"Someone, a young fellow—what's his name?—has been sent by her family to take care of her," the old man explained.

"His name is Sekisuke," O-hisa added. The reflection flashed across the wall again. She went out to the veranda with the basin of hot water she had been using to repair the flaws in her coiffure.

"Sekisuke. He goes along with her. It's a master-servant scene."

"And Miyuki has regained her eyesight?"

"That's right. And won back her place as a samurai's daughter. She goes off down the road dressed as a lady again. It's a bright scene, something like the walk through the cherries in *Sembonzakura*."

The theater was a temporary one in a vacant lot somewhere, and the plays lasted from ten in the morning to eleven at night, sometimes even to past midnight. Since the whole program would really be quite impossible to sit through, it might be best to go toward evening, the manager of the inn suggested, but the old man retorted that he had come purposely for the plays and that they would start out immediately after breakfast. He had brought along the usual lacquer boxes, which made up a large part of his pleasure at the theater, and handed them over with elaborate instructions—there would be this vegetable, that omelet—on what was to be put into them for lunch and dinner.

93

"Well, O-hisa, let's get ourselves ready," he prodded.

"Could you pull this tight, please?" O-hisa turned so that the knot of her sash was toward him. Even before the order came she had set about tying the brocade, its material crisp and crackly as a priest's robe, over a solid-colored kimono so stiff that it seemed on the verge of splitting at the creases.

"Is that tight enough?"

'A little more, please."

O-hisa strained forward, bracing herself from the hip. Sweat came out on the old man's forehead.

"The damned thing refuses to budge. It's almost impossible to tie."

"You were the one who bought it, I believe. Certainly I never approved. It beats me to exhaustion. Tight, uncomfortable."

"But it's a good color, isn't it?" Kaname stood admiringly beside the old man. "I don't quite know what you'd call it, but it's something you don't much see these days."

"A sort of chartreuse, I suppose it would be. It's still used often enough, but the real flavor doesn't come out till it's old and faded like this."

"What's the material?"

"Figured satin, I should say. The old silks are the only ones that crackle this way. There's almost always rayon in the new ones."

Since the theater was within walking distance, they started out on foot, each with his share of lacquer boxes and small packages.

"It's bright enough so that I'll need a parasol." O-hisa, always afraid of sunburn, shaded her face with her hand. The sun came through her fingers brilliant as through red parasol paper, and on down over her delicate palm, with its callus from playing the samisen. The shaded upper part of her face seemed even whiter than her sun-bathed chin.

"There's no point in worrying about an umbrella," the old man said curtly. "You'll be burned black before we get home anyway."

O-hisa did not agree. While they waited in the entrance she took out the cream she had slipped into the bottom of her bag and applied it with soft little pats to her face, neck, wrists, even her ankles. The pains this Kyoto lady took with her fair complexion struck Kaname as at the same time charming and ridiculous. The pleasure-minded old man, however, for all that he seemed to be concerned with just such fine points, showed curiously little sympathy now that he had made his views known.

"We won't be there before eleven." It was O-hisa's turn to prod the old man, who stopped now and then in front of an antique shop.

"What lovely weather!" She looked up into the clear sky as she walked slowly on ahead with Kaname, adding in a low voice, a little wistfully: "On a day like this I'd rather be out looking for spring greens."

"It is a better day for that than for a play."

"I wonder if there are good greens around here."

"I know nothing about this part of the country. I should think there would be plenty in the hills around Kyoto, though."

"There are indeed. Just last month we went out to Yase to look for aster sprouts. We took in a great supply."

"Aster sprouts?"

"He eats them. I looked through the markets in Kyoto, but there were none to be had. The grocers all said the things were too bitter for human consumption."

"Even in Tokyo it's not everybody who can get them down. So you went all the way to Yase after them?"

"We filled a basket this big."

"It's fun to go looking for greens, I suppose, but it's fun too just to wander through a country town on a day like this."

The main road through the town stretched on under the blue sky before them, so clear and serene that they could count the people passing back and forth far into the distance. Even the bicycles tinkling their bells as they moved by seemed calm and unhurried. The town was not an especially remarkable one, but like every town in this part of the country it had its lines of fine earthen walls. The old man had gone into that too: the driving winds and rains farther to the east make it necessary to put up board fences rather than these earthen walls, he found, and the wood, no matter how fine it is,

95

soon turns dark and begins to look dirty. Tokyo is a special problem of course, rebuilt with tin-roofed barracks after the earthquake, but one might expect the small provincial centers around it to have a patina in proportion as they are old. In fact they are gloomy as though overlaid with a coating of soot. Earthquakes and fires are common, and each rebuilding brings characterless houses of cheap imported woods that might better be used for matches, and shabby Western-style buildings that suggest a run-down, end-of-the-line town in the United States. A very old city in the east, the medieval military seat at Kamakura for instance, might not indeed have all the beauty of the ancient capital at Nara if it were moved west, but it would certainly have more repose and grace than it has. The country from Kyoto west has been blessed by nature, and disasters are few; and the earthen walls and tiles of even obscure town houses and farms can make the traveler stop and gaze for a moment. The smaller of the old castle towns have more of this charm than large, modernized cities like Osaka, or even Kyoto, a much less extreme example. With the heart of Kyoto changing so rapidly, one has to go to Wakayama, Sakai, Himeji, Nishinomiya, to find the old cities as they have always been.

As his eye fell on a corner of crumbling wall with white blossoms arching out over the rounded tiles at its ridge, Kaname thought of something else the old man had once said: "People talk about famous places in the east like Shiobara and Hakone, but Japan is a volcanic country and you can find that kind of scenery everywhere. When the *Mainichi* was running its poll for the best eight views in the country, they say, it uncovered more 'lion rocks' than you could count. I don't doubt it a moment. The places really worth going to are the little towns and harbors from here on west."

The island of Awaji showed not very large on the map, and its harbor very possibly consisted of but this one road. You go straight down, the inn manager had said, till you come out at the river, and the theater is in the flats beyond. The rows of houses therefore most probably ended at the river. This may have been the seat of some minor baron a century ago—even then it could hardly have been imposing enough to be called a castle town—and it had probably changed little since. A modern coating goes no farther than the large cities that are a country's arteries, and there are not many such cities anywhere. In an old country with a long tradition, China and Europe as well as Japan—any country, in fact, except a very new one like the United States—the smaller cities, left aside by the flow of civilization, retain the flavor of an earlier day until they are overtaken by catastrophe.

This little harbor, for instance: it had its electric wires and poles, its painted billboards, and here and there a display window, but one could ignore them and find on every side townsmen's houses that might have come from an illustration to a seventeenth-century novel. The earthen walls covered to the eaves with white plaster, the projecting lattice fronts with their solid, generous slats of wood, the heavy tiled roofs held down by round ridge-tiles, the shop signs—"Lacquer," "Soy," "Oil"—in fading letters on fine hardwood grounds, and inside, beyond earth-floored entrances, the shop names printed on dark-blue half-curtains—it was not the old man's remark this time, but every detail brought back—how vividly!—the mood and air of old Japan. Kaname felt as if he were being drunk up into the scene, as if he were losing himself in the clean white walls and the brilliant blue sky. Those walls were a little like the sash around O-hisa's waist: their first luster had disappeared in long years under the fresh sea winds and rains, and bright though they were, their brightness was tempered by a certain reserve, a soft austerity.

Kaname felt a deep repose come over him. "These old houses are so dark you have no idea what's inside."

"Partly it's because the road is so bright." The old man had come up beside them. "The ground here seems almost white."

Kaname thought of the faces of the ancients in the dusk behind their shop curtains. Here on this street people with faces like theater dolls must have passed lives like stage lives. The world of the plays—of O-yumi, Jūrōbei of Awa, the pilgrim O-tsuru, and the rest—must have been just such a town as this. And wasn't O-hisa a part of it? Fifty years ago, a hundred years ago, a woman like her, dressed in the same kimono, was perhaps going down this same street in the spring sun, lunch in hand, on her way to the theater beyond the river. Or perhaps, behind one of these latticed fronts, she was playing "Snow" on her koto. O-hisa was a shade left behind by another age.

## CHAPTER ELEVEN

NATIVES of Awaji say that the puppet theater originated there. In the center of the island there is a village called Ichimura that even now has seven puppet companies. Once there were thirty-six. Ichimura is known as "puppet-town," and its theater goes back, one hardly knows how many centuries, to a certain court nobleman who was banished from Kyoto and came to live in Ichimura, and who in his boredom with country life took to making puppets and manipulating them for his own amusement. The famous Awaji Gennojō family descends from him, it is said. The family still has an impressive estate in the village, and its puppet company goes on tour from Awaji to Shikoku on the south and to western Honshu on the north. But the Gennojō family has no monopoly on the Ichimura puppets. One might say, in fact, with perhaps a little exaggeration, that the whole village is in some way occupied with the puppet theater, as singers and accompanists, puppeteers and stage managers. In busy seasons the people of Ichimura move out to work in the fields, and in slack seasons they fall into puppet companies to tour the island. The Awaji theater is in the truest sense a folk art, an art born long ago of rural tradition.

January and May are the theater months. If one crosses over to Awaji then, one finds plays in the towns and in the fields, all over the island. In the larger towns a building is sometimes borrowed, but for the most part the plays are given half out of doors and under makeshift shelters of logs and rush mats, and when it rains, that is the end of a day's performance. A real puppet madness occasionally seizes the Awaji farmer.

He wanders from house to house with little one-hand marionettes, going through a favorite passage, himself both singer and puppeteer, when someone asks him in; he may even bring his house to ruin with his puppets, and he has been known in an extreme case to go quite insane.

But with the new age and its pressures, even this proud art is dying. The old dolls deteriorate until they can no longer be used, and there is almost no one who can replace them. Only three men still call themselves puppet-makers, Tengu-Hisa and his student Tengu-Ben across the straits in Tokushima, and Yura-Game of Yura on Awaji. Tengu-Hisa, the only real master of the three, is an old man of sixty or seventy. When he dies the old art will probably die with him. Tengu-Ben is in Osaka with the Bunraku puppet theater, but his work is actually limited to repairing old dolls and to retouching their faces; and while in his day old Yura-Game made some fine puppets, the younger Yura-Game is a barber or some such fellow who repairs puppets in his spare time. Since the old puppets are thus as good as irreplaceable, great pains are taken to preserve them. In the summer or just before the New Year broken puppets from all over the island are collected at the puppet-maker's for repairs, and a broken head or two can be had cheaply if one goes to Awaji at the right time, it is said.

The old man had explored the possibility in great detail. "This time I am definitely going to get myself a puppet," he announced.

He had been trying without much success to get an old puppet from the Bunraku theater in Osaka. The Awaji pilgrimage was planned at least partly to let him look for the puppet he had been assured could be found there. He would see a puppet play, he said he would visit the Gennojō family and Yura-Game, and on the way back to Osaka he would cross the straits and visit Tengu-Hisa in Tokushima.

"Unhurried, isn't it? Did you ever see anything quite like it?"

"Unhurried it is, all right," Kaname agreed. He and the old man exchanged glances as they entered the shelter with its rush-matted pit. Relaxed, unhurried—the words quite took in the mood of the place. Once, one day toward the end of an April, he did not remember how long ago, Kaname had gone to the pantomimes at the Mibu Temple in Kyoto. The lazy warmth of spring bathed the temple precincts, and in the stands he felt a pleasant drowsiness come over him. The voices of the children playing outside, the awnings of the little festival shops, the candy shops and the comic-mask shops, shining like stained glass in the sun—all the sounds and impressions from the street and the temple yard melted into the slow, genial sounds of the recitation and the twanging accompaniment on the stage with one quiet, liquid movement. Kaname would find himself drifting off to sleep and pull himself awake; twice, three times, the drowsing off and the quick awakening . . . and again and then again. And each time he opened his eyes the same farce still held the stage, the same slow recital still pushed its way along, the children still played outside, and the lazy sun still reflected from the awnings. A spring day that would never end, he almost felt. . . . It was as if a hundred formless and uncollected dreams were passing through his mind, the dreaming and the waking fused one into the other. . . . Call it a taste of the joys of great peace, call it a transport to some fairyland, it was a feeling of serene removal from the world such as Kaname had not felt since the day he had been taken, still a child, to see the Kagura dancing at the Shrine of the Sea God in the old downtown section of Tokyo.

Here in the puppet theater he felt the mood come over him again. Although the roof and sides were covered with straw mats, irregular chinks where they met admitted rays of sunlight to the pit and the seats around it. Here and there a patch of blue sky showed, or a stretch of waving, rustling grass down toward the river. Where another theater would have been dark with tobacco smoke, this one was fresh as the out-of-doors, and a spring breeze came in over meadows bright with dandelions and the mauve of clover.

In the pit, where rush mats and rows of cushions were laid out on the bare ground, the children of the village had taken over. Noisy games, oranges, candy—it was lively as the playground of a kindergarten, untroubled as a country shrine festival. No one seemed to notice that a play was going on.

"A bit different from what we find in Osaka."

The three of them, boxes in hand, stood for a time looking down at the confusion of the small juvenile kingdom, not trying to move on inside.

"The play must have started. The puppets seem to be moving."

Across the kindergarten in the pit there flickered suggestions of something different in kind from the puppet theater Kaname had seen in Osaka. A world of fantasy, it seemed, childlike in its simplicity and its radiance. The silk backdrop was splashed with morning-glories, and the scene must be the firefly hunt on the River Uji at the beginning of *Morning-Glory Diary,* he decided. A young warrior puppet, Komazawa no doubt, and a beautiful young girl one would take for Miyuki knelt side by side on the deck of a boat, bent one toward the other, fans in hand, whispering of love. Kaname would have expected the scene to be sensuous, erotic; but he could hear neither the singing nor the samisen accompaniment, and the engaging little movements of the puppets suggested an art far removed from the realism of the Bungorō and the Osaka theater. It was almost as if the puppets here were playing with the children in the pit, innocently, unaffectedly.

O-hisa started for the stands. The old man, however, was of the opinion that the puppet stage should be seen from below. "This is what we want," he said, deliberately choosing a place in the open pit.

The spring grass was pleasant enough, but the chill of the raw ground soon crept through the thin mats and cushions.

"I shan't be able to stand up afterwards," said O-hisa, piling up three cushions for herself. "And it's hardly what you would call healthy, either."

"You can't expect comfort at a place like this, and you don't get the feel of the play from up there. And think of the fun you'll have talking about the cold afterwards."

It was evident, though, for all his determination to ignore it, that the old man felt the cold himself. Presently he had saké warming over an alcohol burner.

"We seem to be quite in style. Everyone has boxes."

"Some of them are elaborate enough, too—look at the lacquer-work," said Kaname. "I suppose when everyone automatically goes to the play, everyone automatically takes along the same lunch."

"It used to be that way everywhere. It was in Osaka until not too long ago. In Kyoto you still see old families going out to look at the cherry blossoms, and the houseboy walking on ahead with the lunch and the saké. When they arrive at wherever they're going, they hire a kettle to heat the saké, and when they finish, they put what's left back in the bottle and take it home for cooking. A Tokyo man will tell you that shows how tightfisted they are in Kyoto, but when you think about it, it's not a bad idea to carry along your own lunch and not have to take your chances with a restaurant. At least you know what you're eating."

The audience was mostly in the pit, gathered here and there in little knots, each knot beginning its own celebration. There were few men, perhaps because it was still early in the day. The village wives and daughters, usually with a few children, some with babes in arms, formed their ranks around the lunch boxes quite as though they had taken up housekeeping, quite untroubled by what was happening on the stage. The bustle and the clutter were immense.

Stew and saké were on sale at the refreshment stand, which was patronized by a few of the parties. Most of the spectators, however, had their own lunches in the impressive boxes that had caught the old man's eye. It must have been rather like this at Asuka-yama and the other popular cherry resorts in Tokyo, Kaname thought, before the old system, the system of the centuries of isolation, began to break down. The elaborate lacquerware had always seemed to him a luxury whose day was past, but here for the first time he saw it as useful and unaffected. Indeed, now that he thought of it, the lacquer did go well with the theater lunch, with the pale tones of its omelets and rice balls. There were lively reds and whites throughout the theater, and somehow the food was more appetizing by virtue of the color effect. Japanese food is meant to be looked at and not eaten, people sometimes say. Perhaps they are right if they are making fun of the formal banquet carefully laid out on its trays. But here the colors were more than only pleasant to look at; they worked on the appetite, made even the unremarkable rice and pickles seem a little more exciting.

"It's the saké and the cold that do it," the old man said, getting up and excusing himself. He had already been outside two or three times.

But the most in distress was O-hisa. Knowing what sort of place it would be, she had made what preparations she could to get through the day without incident. Her attempts to forestall a crisis only acted as a stimulant, however, and too, with the cold creeping up her spine, she had made the mistake of joining the old man in a cup or two. Presently the crisis was immediate.

She got up. "Excuse me, but where . . ."

Kaname went out to explore and came back frowning. "It will never do for you." The facilities were in fact limited to two or three buckets, quite out in the open and used without inhibition by men and women alike.

"What should I do?"

"What are you worried about?" the old man broke in. "If they stare at you, stare right back at them."

"But I don't think I could manage—standing."

"Don't women stand in Kyoto?"

"I know at least one who never has."

O-hisa went out to look for a restaurant in the neighborhood. It was nearly an hour before she came back. She had walked past the restaurants and found them all a little hard to go into, not the sort of restaurants she liked, and she had found herself at the inn and had hired a rickshaw to bring her back. She wondered what the other young women did (the old women, of course, were up to anything), whether they really managed with those open buckets. As she was turning the problem over in her mind, a disturbance broke out behind them.

A housewife, posting herself squarely in the aisle, had helped her small boy undo his buttons so that he could relieve himself. It was as though the plumbing had burst, and even the old man was a little upset.

"Things are getting primitive. Practically in our lunch, too."

Meanwhile, unaffected by the confusion, the play took its course and singers came and went. Perhaps a little heady from saké taken so early in the day and from the conversation buzzing so violently around him, Kaname saw it only as a succession of flickering images quite detached from any narrative. Not that he was bored or annoyed. The sensation was rather the pleasant one of pickling in a warm bath, or perhaps of sleeping fitfully on a warm morning, a sweet, unhurried, languorous sensation. While he watched the play in this absent mood, Miyuki and Komazawa apparently parted at Akashi, and several more scenes passed, and the action reached the shelter at Hamamatsu; but the sunlight showed no sign of fading, and through the chinks in the mats the blue sky still shone as happily as in the morning. It hardly seemed necessary to worry about the plot. Just to lose oneself in the movements of the puppets was enough, and the disorderliness of the audience was no hindrance. Rather the myriad noises and myriad colors combined into a brightness, a liveliness, like a kaleidoscope pointed into the sun, and the eye took from them an over-all harmony.

"Unhurried." Kaname tried the word again.

"But the puppets are remarkable. And the man handling Miyuki is not bad at all."

"It might be better if it were even a little more primitive."

"This sort of thing is fairly standard wherever you see it. The lines are the same and the action follows along."

"And the Awaji singing?"

"Some people say there's a difference, but I've never been able to see it myself. Osaka and Awaji sound pretty much alike to me."

To conform to a type, to be the captive of a form, means the decadence of an art, it is sometimes said. But what of folk arts like this puppet theater—have they not become what they are with the help of hard, fixed standards? The heavy-toned old country plays, in a sense, have in them the work of the race. Generation after generation of gifted performers has built each item in the repertoire to a standardization of property and action, handed on so carefully that by following its prescriptions the amateur can mount the singer's platform and bring forth a fair copy of the play, and the spectators as they watch can make the association in their minds with the great names whose work is there. Sometimes

at a country inn one sees a sort of amateur theatrical put
on by children. The instruction has been good, and the
performers have learned well—one wonders how they
can have learned so well. Perhaps it is that the old theater,
unlike the modern theater with all its erratic individual
flights, provides a guide and a reference to which women
and children can turn, and makes the teaching and the
learning easy. In the days before motion pictures, there
was thus a happy substitute for them: a few hands and a
little equipment, and a puppet theater could be put together to wander lightly over the country. It must have
been a deep comfort to the farmers, this theater—one
cannot know what a comfort and a diversion. How
thoroughly the old theater must have penetrated into the
corners of the country, one thinks, how deeply its roots
must have sunk themselves into the life of the farms!

Kaname had seen the parts of *Morning-Glory Diary*
that everyone sees, the last encounter at the inn and the
separation at the river crossing. He was therefore familiar with lines like "One year, firefly-hunting on the
River Uji," and "Weeping, we await a sailing wind at
Akashi," but he had never before actually seen the firefly
hunt on the Uji, or the farewell at Akashi, or the present
scene in the shelter at Hamamatsu. While it resembled a
historical play in many ways, it fortunately lacked the
contorted plot and the warrior's cruelty that so charac-
terize the historical drama. Rather it moved forward with
the simple brightness that one associates with the genre
theater, with even a touch of light humor. Kaname did
not know what period was supposed to be represented,
or whether the love story was based on historical fact. He
had heard somewhere that the hero, Komazawa, was
modeled on the seventeenth-century Confucian scholar
Kumazawa Banzan. Somehow, though, the play seemed
to take one back to an earlier time, to the civil wars of
the fifteenth and sixteenth centuries, or to the Muro-
machi Shogunate before them. Indeed, there were
touches that seemed to suggest Heian, the great period
of the court nobility—the warrior sending an old folksong to the maiden, and the maiden singing it to the accompaniment of the koto, the old Heian zither; or the
maiden followed about by a faithful and diligent nurse
named Asaka, "Faint Perfume." But while one was thus

taken back to the far past, one had at the same time a feeling that the action was extremely near at hand, popular, plebeian. Asaka dressed as a pilgrim, singing her song, seemed to be close to these people, a close acquaintance. One would not be surprised to encounter now and then a woman dressed in the same clothes and singing the same song in the streets hereabouts. The puppet theater must seem as near and familiar to the native of this western part of the country as it seemed foreign to the easterner from Tokyo.

"But we could have had a better play," the old man remarked suddenly, as though he had remembered something. *"The Lady Tamamo* or *Song of Ise,* for instance. You see things in them you never see in Osaka, they say."

Passages that have been cut from the Osaka plays as gruesome or immodest are still shown at Awaji in their pure, untrimmed form, and it was to those eccentricities that the old man referred. *The Lady Tamamo,* for instance, is usually shown at Osaka in three acts only, but at Awaji it is played straight through from the prologue, and the nine-tailed fox, having killed the Lady Tamamo, is shown eating her entrails—wads of red cotton apparently. In *Song of Ise* the slaughter of the ten is shown most graphically, with arms and legs strewn about the stage. Or, in a somewhat more playful vein, a devil with a most monstrously large head arrives to be exorcised at the climax of *Mount Óe.*

"That's what we need. None of this tameness. Tomorrow they do *Mount Imose*—something like that would be worth seeing."

"But I like this one well enough. Possibly because this is the first time I've seen it through from the beginning."

Kaname knew little about the finer points of handling puppets. He did feel, though, the roughness of this performance in comparison with the Osaka puppet theater; it could only be called countrified, he had to conclude. Part of this effect was no doubt due to the puppets themselves, to their features and their clothes. The faces were stiff, hard, at a distance from humanity. In Osaka the heroine would have had a round, gentle face; here she had a long, cold face, a high nose like a proud Kyoto carving or one of the dolls brought out in the spring for the Doll Festival. The face of the villain was violently red and evil, the face of a devil or an apparition rather than that of a man. Then too the puppets (this was particularly true of the heads) were a good deal larger than those in Osaka, the principal ones, indeed, as large as a child of seven or eight. The native of Awaji says that the Osaka puppets are too small, that it is not possible to catch the finer expressions from the Osaka stage. He objects also to the powdered faces of the Osaka puppets. The Osaka craftsmen, in their efforts to produce the effect of the human skin, leave a coating of powder over the paint, while at Awaji the sheen is purposely brought out by careful polishing, and the Osaka style is scorned as gauche and crude. Indeed, one has to admit that the Awaji puppets are expressive, their eyes in particular being active and versatile. The principal puppets can move their eyes up and down and to the right and left, can express red-eyed anger and pale-eyed astonishment. The Osaka puppet has no such skill. The lady puppet in fact is unable to use her eyes at all, while at Awaji, one is proudly told, even she can open and close them at will.

In its general dramatic effect the Osaka performance seemed to Kaname superior; but here at Awaji the audience apparently paid less attention to the play itself than to the puppets. The puppets they watched as a parent would watch a performing child, dwelling carefully and fondly on each gesture. While the Osaka theater, subsidized by the great Shōchiku theater company, could afford certain fineries, however, the Awaji theater, the hobby of farmers, had to get by as best it could. The ornaments and the clothes were shabby, and both Miyuki and Komazawa looked more than a little threadbare.

But the old man, with his fondness for old clothes, liked them. "Much better than in Osaka," he said. He had for some time been turning an envious eye on the puppets' clothing, calling attention to the choicer articles, here a stiff mohair sash, there a yellow Hachijō kimono. "It used to be this way in Osaka, but lately they've gone gaudy. It's all right, I suppose, for them to get new costumes every season, but it's a sign of decay when they start using muslin prints and gold dust. Puppets are like Noh actors. The older their clothes are, the better."

Miyuki and her companion started off down the Tōkaidō Highway, and the long day came toward a close. It was quite dark when the curtain fell on the final roadside scene of *Morning-Glory Diary*. The stands began to fill, the clutter and disorder of the day gave way to the air of an evening at the theater, and small dinner parties took shape all through the building. Bare hundred-watt bulbs hung here and there, lighting up the place well enough, but giving off fearsome glare. The stage too was lighted with bare bulbs hung from above—no such theatrical frills here as footlights and floodlights. As the next play began, the dolls' faces grew still shinier, and Jūjirō and Hatsugiku gave off such a radiance that it was quite impossible to see what they really looked like.

The changes of singers began to bring on near-professionals. From one side of the hall someone shouted: "Be quiet, everybody. He's from my village. Good, isn't he?" And from somewhere else: "Let's have no more of that. Ours is a whole lot better." A good half of the audience, evidently aroused by the saké, took the part of one side or the other, and the competition between village and village grew intense as the evening progressed. At the poetic climax the loudest of the appreciators became quite intoxicated with emotion. "It's too much," they cried in tear-laden voices. The puppeteers, too, seemed to have had a cup or two. Their bloodshot eyes could have been overlooked had it not been for the remarkable way they had of hanging over the dolls—particularly the lady dolls—at crucial junctures. The same mannerisms are seen in Osaka, of course, but these men would have been striking enough anyway in their formal stage dress, their faces burned black from the days in the fields and flushed from liquor. The cries from the audience ("It is too much!") urged them on until, drunk with their art, they were following the movements of the puppets with their bodies, the voluptuousness of it plain on their faces. Presently, too, some of the capers the old man had missed in *Morning-Glory Diary* began to appear. Yojirō, the monkey-trainer in *The Love of Oshun and Dembei*, stepped outside the house to relieve himself before going to bed, and a dog wandered up from somewhere and backed away with the end of his loincloth in its mouth.

It was ten o'clock before the last number, given conspicuous play on the program for its Osaka singer, came on the stage. Shortly after it began, there was a disturbance. A man in a dark-blue jacket buttoned high at the throat, a road-gang foreman he might have been, suddenly jumped up in the pit from the party of five or six he had been drinking with and began challenging someone in the stands to come out and fight. There had been some rancor in the audience, which was divided between supporters of the Osaka singer and local patriots who resented him, and one of the catcalls had particularly annoyed the boss-like gentleman. "Come on out, damn you. Come out," he shouted, and made as if to plunge into the stands. His friends tried to quiet him, but he struck a pose like one of the guardian warriors at a temple gate and continued to bellow, while the rest of the audience shouted their resentment at the noise. The singer from Osaka was quite lost in the turmoil.

# CHAPTER TWELVE

"WELL, Kaname, we'll see you later."

"Take care of yourself. I only hope the weather holds for you. And don't let O-hisa get sunburned."

O-hisa laughed softly, her dark front teeth showing under her deep cone-shaped sunshade. "Give my best to Misako," she said.

It was eight o'clock in the morning. Kaname was taking the boat for Kobe, and the other two, in pilgrim's dress, were ready to start on around the island.

"Do take care of yourselves. When will you be back in Kyoto?"

"I really don't know. All thirty-three temples would be a few too many, I'm afraid. We'll have to cut some of them out. I do want to cross over to Tokushima, though, and go home from there."

"And you're bringing home an Awaji puppet, remember."

"Come up to Kyoto and I'll show it to you. I'll find you a good one this time."

"I'll be up around the end of the month in any case. I have a few things to tend to."

Kaname stood on deck waving his hat as the ship pulled away. The pious Buddhist aphorism written in large characters on the sections of O-hisa's sunshade (part of her pilgrim's equipment) gradually faded away: "For the benighted the illusions of the world. For the enlightened the knowledge that all is vanity. In the beginning there was no east and west. Where then is there a north and south?" It seemed to him, as he watched them there on the dock with their sunshades in the growing distance, that between the two of them there was indeed "no east and west" in spite of the thirty years' difference in their ages, that they were only another well-matched couple off on a pilgrimage. Presently, to a distant tinkling of bells, they turned and started off. The retreating figures made Kaname think of a line from the pilgrim's canticle they had practiced so earnestly with the innkeeper the evening before: "Hopefully we take the path from afar to the temple where blooms the flower of the good law." Kaname, audience for the rehearsal, had picked up the proper rhythms and intonations himself. The old man had with some regret come back early from *Mount Imose,* the day's play, and he and O-hisa had spent the evening from nine to twelve immersed in canticles and sutras. The canticle floated into Kaname's mind alternately with the image of O-hisa as she had started out that morning, the innkeeper helping her into straw sandals, her wrists and ankles bound in shiny white silk after the fashion of pilgrims. He had come along with them for one evening, and the one evening had grown to two and then three. Partly of course it was the puppet plays that had kept him on, but doubtless it was partly too his interest in the relationship between the old man and O-hisa. A sensitive woman, a woman with ideas, can only get more troublesome and less likable with the years. Surely, then, one does better to fall in love with the sort of woman one can cherish as a doll. Kaname had no illusions about his ability to imitate the old man; but still, when he thought of his own family affairs, of that perpetual knowing countenance and of the endless disagreements, the old man's life—off to Awaji appointed like a doll on the stage, accompanied

110

by a doll, in search of an old doll to buy—seemed to suggest a profound spiritual peace reached without training and without effort. If only he could follow the old man's example, Kaname thought.

The weather was flawless still, but apparently there were not many with time for excursions. The ship, a pleasure steamer with leisurely rows of special-class rooms, was almost empty. He had his choice of the Western-style rooms on the second deck or the Japanese-style rooms below. Stretching out on the straw mats in one of the Japanese rooms with his handbag for a pillow, he looked up at the ceiling. The room was deserted but for him. Waves danced and shimmered across the ceiling, the serenity of spring on the Inland Sea reflected blue into the softly lighted room. Now and then, as the shadow of an island passed, a smell compounded of flowers and the tide seemed to press stealthily in on him. Kaname was always careful about his clothes and he was not used to traveling; and even for a trip planned to take no more than two or three days he had brought along several changes of clothing. He had on a kimono for the return trip. Suddenly, however, he thought of something, and taking advantage of the solitude, he quickly changed to a gray flannel suit. Then he went to sleep. Several hours later he awoke to the sound of the anchor chain on the deck above.

It was only eleven in the morning when the ship docked at Hyogo, to the west of the main Kobe harbor. Kaname did not start for home immediately, but went to the Oriental Hotel and for the first time since before his departure for Awaji had something rich and foreign to eat. He spent twenty minutes over a glass of Benedictine, and still felt a little heady when his cab pulled up in front of Mrs. Brent's house, high up in the hills behind the harbor. He pressed the bell at the gate with the tip of his umbrella.

"Hello, hello. Why the baggage?"

"I just got off the ship."

"The ship?"

"I was on Awaji for a couple of days. Is Louise in?"

"She may still be in bed."

"The Madam?"

The boy pointed to the end of the hall. There, at the

111

head of the steps leading down to the garden, Mrs. Brent sat with her back toward him. Usually when she heard his voice she brought her hundred and seventy or eighty pounds noisily down the stairs to greet him, but today she only sat and stared down into the garden, not even turning around. The house might have been built when the ports were opened, around the middle of the last century. High-ceilinged, dark, sedate, it must once have been a fine mansion, but it had been allowed to run to seed until now it suggested a haunted house. Rank and wasted though it was, however, the back garden was flooded with a radiance of May foliage, and the sun reflected from the Madam's curly brown hair and turned a lock of it here and there to the brightest silver.

"What's the trouble? What's she staring at?"

"She hasn't been feeling well. As a matter of fact, she's been crying."

"Crying?"

"She got a cable yesterday evening saying her brother was dead, and she's been this way ever since. Hasn't had a drink all morning. You might say something to her, if you don't mind."

Kaname went up behind Mrs. Brent. "Hello, Mrs. Brent. Is it true?—they tell me your brother is dead."

In the shade of a great purple-flowered sandalwood tree, mint and weeds were growing in the wildest profusion. The mint was left untouched for Mrs. Brent to use with roast mutton or punch, and the rims of her eyes as she stared into the garden, a white lace handkerchief pressed to her face, looked as though some of the pungence might have eaten its way into them.

"I'm terribly sorry to hear it."

"It's kind of you to say so."

A tear drew a line of light down from her sagging eyelids, folded in layer after layer of wrinkles. Kaname had heard that foreign women tend to weep, but this was the first time he had actually seen one of them weeping. Somehow it struck him as intensely sad, just as a foreign song with whose melody he was still not entirely familiar could strike him with the force of its melancholy.

"Where did your brother die?"

"In Canada."

"How old was he?"

"Forty-eight, forty-nine, fifty—something like that, I think."

"He was still young then. Will you have to go to Canada?"

"I've decided not to. There's nothing I could do."

"How long has it been since you last saw him?"

"Twenty years or so—it was when I was in London in 1909. We've written letters since, but that was the last time."

How old would the Madam herself be, then? Older than the brother, of course. Kaname had known her now for more than ten years. She had had two houses on the Bluff—the foreign quarter—before the great earthquake ruined Yokohama, and five or six girls in each; and she had had this house in Kobe too, a sort of branch villa as it were, and houses in Shanghai and Hong Kong. Traveling back and forth between China and Japan, she had for a time ruled over a rather extensive empire. But presently, as her health and energy failed, her business began to crumble away. Mrs. Brent herself said that since 1918 the Japanese had started taking over trade and forcing out foreign firms, and that the reckless tourists of the early days had stopped coming. Kaname felt, however, that those were not the only causes for her decline. When he had first known her she was not the ruin he saw now. Born in Yorkshire, she had received a fine education at some girls' school or other, she was always pleased to say. She knew not a word of Japanese, even though she had been in Japan more than ten years, and while her girls fell into the pidgin of the foreign concessions, she persisted in using pure English—indeed, making it a point to bring in as many difficult words and idioms as she could. Her German and French too were fluent. She had the dignity that went with her position, she had a lively personality, and she still preserved something of the charm of her youth. Kaname marveled at the ability of foreign women to resist age. But the time came when her strength of character began to slacken, her memory failed, and her ability to control people quite left her, and soon it was almost as if he could see her aging before his eyes. In the old days she would buttonhole a customer and boast of some foreign count who had slipped into one of her places the evening before, or, an English-language newspaper spread in front of her, she would launch forth on the subject of England's Far Eastern policies, mystifying her customers with deep and subtle questions. The old bluff had disappeared, however, and only a propensity for lies remained. It had become a disease, almost too obvious and easily detected a disease.

That such a forceful individual should have degenerated to this seemed to Kaname most remarkable. He suspected that drink was responsible. As her wits grew duller and her body grew puffier, her consumption of liquor climbed steadily. She had once been able to keep herself under tight control even when she was drunk, but now she wheezed untidily about the house from early in the morning, and, according to the houseboy, she drank herself into a stupor two or three times a month. A model case of high blood pressure, she might fall over dead almost any minute, one felt. It could hardly be expected, then, that her house would prosper, whatever business conditions in general might be. The cleverer of the girls ran away after piling up debts, the cook and the amah cheated on the whisky bill. In the good days she had hired only pure blonde western-European girls from the English concession, but these last two or three years the roster had narrowed down to Eurasians and White Russians, and never more than two or three of them at a time.

"You can't help being sad, of course, but won't you make yourself sick if you go on crying this way? It's not like you. Pull yourself together, have a drink. People have to accept these things."

"Thank you. You are most kind. But he was my only brother. Everyone has to die, I know. Everyone has to die some time. But still . . ."

"Exactly right. The only thing to do is accept it."

There is a type of old and unwanted geisha, found often at country teahouses, who will seize a customer she barely knows and pour out all her misfortunes for him, who intoxicates herself with the cheapest sentimentality. The Madam here, one had to admit, was of the type. Undoubtedly she was sad, but in her desire for attention she was striking too many poses. Still, for all its artificiality, Kaname could not but be moved at the sorrow of the massive foreign woman. Her tears were the tears of the country geisha, and yet he felt his own eyes misting over.

"Please forgive me. Here I've upset you with all this weeping, when I really should wait till I'm alone."

"Nothing of the sort. But do be careful. There's no point in making yourself sick just because your brother is dead."

Kaname felt a little ashamed of himself. He knew that he would never be so forward with a Japanese woman. What could account for it? Perhaps he had come expecting to see Louise and had been caught off guard by this encounter? Perhaps the fine weather had got the better of him? The scent of the mint and the radiance of the spring leaves had gone to his head? Or possibly English was especially suited for sad occasions? In Japanese he had never spoken half so sweetly and softly to his wife or his dead mother.

"What happened? Did the Madam get hold of you?" Louise asked when she received him on the second floor.

"It was a little embarrassing. I don't like tearful conversations, but I couldn't run off with her crying right in my face."

Louise giggled. "I thought so. She isn't satisfied until she's wept a little for everyone who comes in."

"But it can't be entirely an act."

"Well, after all, her brother did die, and she must feel sad about it. You've been to Awaji?"

"Yes."

"And who was with you?"

"My father-in-law and his lady friend."

"Whose lady friend did you say? Not that I don't know."

"My father-in-law's, I said. I do like her a little, though."

"Then why did you come here?"

"I need someone to cheer me up now that I've seen how well other people get on together."

"How flattering!"

Had someone who did not know the two been listening from the next room, he could hardly have guessed from

115

the woman's speech that she had bobbed chestnut hair and brown eyes. Her Japanese was excellent. Even now, when Kaname closed his eyes, he could imagine from her tone and accent and choice of words that he was in a country restaurant with a barmaid beside him serving saké. A trace of something exotic gave her speech a little the rising accent of northern Japan, and with her frightful glibness she sounded like a too knowing wench who has worked her way around the provinces. She would never have suspected it, of course.

And when, after closing his eyes and letting Louise's chattering create what moods it would, Kaname opened them again and looked about him, he found the scene quite startling. There was Louise on the chair in front of the dressing-table, a brocade pajama top, patterned after a mandarin robe, coming barely to her hips, below that only her carefully powdered legs and a pair of pale-yellow high-heeled French slippers, their toes pointed like the prows of two little submarines. Indeed, almost her whole body was covered with a delicate coating of white powder—Kaname had had to wait more than a half-hour for her to finish powdering herself after her bath. She said that her mother had some Turkish blood, and that she felt she had to hide the darkness of her complexion. As a matter of fact, though, it had been the dark glow of her skin, with its faint suggestion of impurity, that had attracted Kaname. Once he had brought a friend here, and the friend, just back from France, had said: "You would have a hard time finding a woman like her even in Paris. Who would expect to see one wandering around Kobe?"

Kaname had first come to the house in Kobe two or three years before, quite on the impulse of a moment, because he had been received in Mrs. Brent's Yokohama houses in spite of his being Japanese. Louise on that first visit came out with a couple of other girls to greet him and to have a glass of champagne at his expense. She had been in Kobe only three months, she said. She was born in Poland, had been driven from her home by the war, and had lived in Russia, Manchuria, and Korea, picking up new languages along the way. She talked to the other two girls with no difficulty in Russian. "If I ever went to Paris I would be talking like a French-

116

man in a month," she boasted. Apparently she had something of a genius for languages, and she alone of the girls was able to handle Mrs. Brent or a drunken American in English. But that she should have mastered Japanese in such a short time—one minute she would be singing Slavic songs to the balalaika or the guitar, the next she would be at "Song of the Yalu River" or "Song of the Yasuki Boatman," almost with the skill of a professional minstrel. Kaname, who had always spoken to her in English, had discovered this sinister talent only recently.

It was foolish, however, to have expected that a woman in her profession would tell the truth about her past. Later he learned from the houseboy that she was really the Eurasian daughter of a Russian and a Korean, and that she occasionally had letters from her mother in Seoul. Her linguistic accomplishments and her facility with "Song of the Yalu River" thus became a little more understandable. Among all the lies she had told, though, he wondered if her statement the first time they met that she was eighteen years old might not have been near the truth. Even now she looked no more than twenty. Her speech and her actions were precocious out of all proportion to her physical development, almost inevitably the case with young girls of her exotic origins.

Kaname, who had never really established himself with a mistress but had made it a practice to shift his attentions about, had, in the two or three years since he met her, come only to Louise for relief from the barrenness of his life with Misako. Of all the women he had known, Louise was the most skillful at satisfying the particular need that his unhappy marriage created. Had anyone asked about the attachment, he would have said that he found it safest for secret debauchery to go to a house that rarely admitted Japanese, that Mrs. Brent's was cheaper and less time-consuming than a Japanese teahouse, that after he and a woman had been behaving like animals it was somehow easier for them to forget, less damaging to their pride, when they were foreigners to each other. Indeed, he had almost convinced himself that those were his reasons.

But, for all that he tried to think of her as no more significant than a beautiful, furry, four-legged beast, Kaname felt in her something that suggested the gladness and exuberance of certain Lamaist statues. He knew with painful sureness that he would not find her easy to give up. She was far more considerate, more painstaking, than those self-styled geisha who, surrounded by pink walls and pinned-up photographs of Hollywood stars and perhaps of Suzuki Emmei and Okada Yoshiko,[1] sought to delight the senses of their customers with pedicures and perfumed feet. Frequently, though never out of spite, Kaname would start off in comfortable sports clothes on "errands" in Kobe after Misako had left for Suma, and toward evening he would come back with a few packages in Kobe wrappings. He followed the teachings of Kaibara Ekiken, the seventeenth-century wise man—though for reasons quite opposite to those advanced by Ekiken—and chose the early afternoon for his pleasures. Going home in the daylight took away the unpleasantness of the aftertaste and made it possible to pass the adventure off in the spirit of an afternoon walk.

Only one thing bothered him: the smell of Louise's powder, a particularly strong and stubborn smell. It seemed to sink deep into his skin, it permeated his clothes, it even spread through the taxi when he left and overwhelmed the room when he got home. Aside from the question of whether Misako knew about his flirtation or not, it seemed to Kaname somehow a breach of etiquette to bring another woman's scent home to his wife, granted that she was hardly his wife any more. He sometimes suspected, as a matter of fact, that Misako was not going to Suma at all but had found a convenient nest somewhere nearer. Although he did feel a certain curiosity, it was never aggressive enough to make him investigate. Rather he made it a point to leave things in doubt, and he wanted his own movements left in doubt. Before he put on his clothes in Louise's room, therefore, he always had the boy draw a bath. The powder had the tenaciousness of a strong hair-oil, and he had to scrub himself raw to get rid of it. Sometimes he felt that her skin had enveloped him like an acrobat's tights. He rather wished he could

---

[1] Japanese movie stars of the 1920's. Suzuki recently made an unsuccessful attempt to break into politics. Okada, the Mary Pickford of Japan, is now in Moscow, where she is said to be writing propaganda.—Tr.

leave it on—and this he had to accept as evidence that he was fonder of her than he would admit.

*"Prosit! A votre santé,"* said Louise, raising a bright amber-colored glass to her lips. She always said there was no decent champagne in the place, and overcharged him thirty per cent or so on the Dry Monopole she secretly stored for herself. "Have you thought about what I asked you?"

"I haven't quite got around to it."

"But what are you going to do? Tell me now."

"I can't yet. That's what I haven't got around to."

"I do get tired of it, honestly, saying you haven't got around to it. Remember what I said the other day? A thousand yen will be enough."

"I heard you."

"Then why don't you do something? You said if it was only a thousand yen you might be able to."

"Did I say that?"

"Liar! You know you did. That's why I don't like Japanese."

"I'm so sorry. You must forgive me for being Japanese. What ever happened to the rich American you went to Nikko with?"

"That's not what we're talking about. You're even stingier than I thought. And you would give almost anything to one of those geisha girls."

"Really, if you think I'm that rich, you're wrong. A thousand yen is a lot of money."

This sort of thing took the place with Louise of the more common varieties of bedroom playfulness. At first she had said that she owed the Madam two thousand yen and that she wanted him to pay that off and set her up in a house of her own. Recently, however, she had changed her story, and now she needed only a thousand and could give her note for the rest.

"You do like me, don't you? You do, don't you?"

"Mmm."

"You could be a little more enthusiastic. You really are fond of me, aren't you?"

"I really am."

"Then you should be willing to give me a thousand. If you don't, I'll stop being nice to you. Now, then. Will you or won't you?"

119

"I will, I will. You needn't work yourself into a rage."

"When will you?"

"I'll bring the money next time I come."

"You really will this time? You aren't lying?"

"Well, you never can tell about us Japanese."

"Damn! Just you remember to bring the money. If you don't, no more. You get nothing more from me. I don't want to be in this dirty business all my life, and I'm only asking you to help me. There aren't many who've had it as hard as I have."

Louise took on the manner of a melodramatic actress of the new school. With wide, tragic, tear-laden eyes, she told how insufferable this life was for a person of her quality; she described her unhappy mother, waiting day after day for her to be free; she cursed heaven and damned man. She had had stage experience, and as a dancer she could rival Pavlova. She was different from the other girls, and it was really shameful to waste her talents in a place like this. If she could only get to Paris or Los Angeles she could take care of herself splendidly. Or if one had in mind a more staid way of earning a living, surely someone with her linguistic genius would be useful as a secretary or stenographer to an executive somewhere. Would he help her? Would he introduce her to a movie producer or to a foreign businessman? That and say a hundred or a hundred fifty a month to fill out her earnings would be quite enough. She would need no more.

"It costs you fifty or sixty yen every time you come here, doesn't it? You would really be saving money."

"They say it takes a thousand a month to keep a foreign wife. Do you really think you could get by on a hundred and fifty with your expensive tastes?"

"I could. I'm not like most foreign women. I could earn a hundred, and all together I'd have two hundred and fifty, wouldn't I? Just try me. I'll show you how well I can manage. I won't come coaxing for spending-money and new clothes like other women. It's this business that gives you wrong ideas about me. If you think I have expensive tastes you're very, very wrong. I don't like to brag, but really I do think if I had a house of my own there isn't a woman in the world who could touch me when it came to saving money."

120

"And supposing after I pay all your debts you whisk yourself off to Siberia?"

Louise made a face and beat her feet against the mattress in her chagrin. Kaname rather enjoyed putting her off, but he could not deny that her proposal interested him. She was not the sort of girl who would want to stay long in one place, and he was quite sure, joking aside, that one day she would run away, to Harbin perhaps. That, however, might be rather a relief. What bothered him more was the thought of how complicated it would be to set up a mistress. Louise said that she would be satisfied with a rented Japanese house as long as it had Western furniture, but somehow, even assuming that she could to outward appearances give up her luxuries and take to minding her accounts like an admirable housewife, the picture of her coming into a narrow little room through an ill-fitting door and walking across the puffy insubstantiality of badly made floor matting, her bobbed head emerging from a wifely cotton kimono—somehow the picture had its disenchanting aspects. Kaname at first treated her advances as of no more consequence than those pleasantries a man will embark on when he is trying to be attractive to women, but presently it began to seem that Louise took them more seriously. Her earnestness might well carry him farther than he wanted to go.

The dramatic bill of complaints, however, with its straining and its storming, contained enough comedy to dispel the threat. The shutters were drawn, and the noonday sun of the late spring shone red through the cracks as though stained glass, bringing out the objects in the room in dim outline and lighting up the body of this powdered Kangiten, this Goddess of Joy, a faint pink. Her words poured forth with that faint north-country accent, her hands rose and fell, her hips squirmed. The effect was much less one of tragedy than of aggressive, noisy vitality. Kaname felt most reluctant to interrupt the performance. If only she had on the traditional blue bib, he thought, she would resemble no one so much as Kintarō, the ruddy boy wonder of stage and legend. It was not easy to keep from laughing.

At precisely four thirty as instructed, the boy drew his bath.

"When will you come again?"

"Next Wednesday or so, possibly."

"You'll bring the money?"

"I'll bring the money." The electric fan cool against his bare back, Kaname stepped into his underwear. He affected a certain briskness, covering the distaste he felt at his own coldness, at his tendency to look upon the day's affair as a closed cash transaction.

"You won't forget?"

"I'll bring it." And as he put his hand on the doorknob he said to himself: "I'll not come again."

"I will certainly not come again." Each time he was seen to the door and into a waiting cab by the boy, Kaname made the same resolution, and as he turned to look back at Louise, blowing a kiss from the door, he secretly said good-by forever. But, strangely, the resolution never lasted three days. By the fifth or seventh day the desire to see her again was quite out of control, and no matter what the complications, back he came running to Kobe. Longing before and revulsion after—this flying between extremes was of course not limited to his relations with Louise. He had felt much the same thing with geisha he had known well. But in Louise's case the extremes were farther apart. There must in the final analysis be a physical reason for it—Louise must be a stronger liquor than any of the others. In the days when he still believed what she told him, the idea of her Western birth—and in that he was no different from most young Japanese men—had drawn him to her with a special fascination. Louise's best points, one might say, were that she was fully aware of the attraction and took great care not to show her real color, and that, given this need to deceive, her body and skin and features made it possible for her to carry the deceit off. Kaname admired the natural golden brown of her skin, but even so he was unwilling to break the spell of the white coating, and he had never asked her to take it off. "You would have a hard time finding a woman like her even in Paris." With the impression left by his friend's remark still a strong one, he found something of his longing for Europe satisfied in his relations with Louise. He had had any number of opportunities to go to Europe. Inertia and timidity, however, had always led him to think up obstacles in the way of the trip; and as some of the longing was satisfied, the enthusiasm for

Europe subsided. It made him a little sad sometimes, but then he congratulated himself that he had got over the matter with the least possible inconvenience.

Kaname raised his right hand to his face. For some reason, he did not know why, the smell of Louise's powder always seemed to penetrate deepest into the palm of his right hand and to stay there longest when he had his bath. Lately he had taken to leaving it unwashed, to going home with the voluptuous secret clasped there in his hand.

"Will I really be able to stay away this time?" he asked himself. In his younger days, from an over-strong sense of virtue and propriety, he had dreamed of steady devotion to one woman, and even now, when he could hardly deny that he was being a little wanton and when, anyway, there was no call for scruples and inhibitions, he could not drive that dream from his mind. He rather admired men who could turn from their wives with decision and find consolation in more satisfactory women, and he thought sometimes that if he had been capable of following their example things could somehow have been patched up between him and Misako. He neither boasted of this particular quirk of his nor apologized for it. He sometimes interpreted it to himself, however, less as a hard sense of duty than as a pandering to his own laziness and a fussy prudishness. To keep for a lifetime companion a woman with whom he did not feel half—not a quarter—the delight he felt when he embraced a woman of a different nation and a different race, a woman whom he encountered, so to speak, only at scattered points along the way—surely that was an intolerable dislocation.

## CHAPTER THIRTEEN

My dear Kaname:

*Our trip after we left you went quite as we had planned it. We returned on the 25th of last month. Your most esteemed letter of the 29th arrived yesterday and was read with the deepest astonishment. Though I was aware that Misako's character left something to be desired, I must say that it was not for this piece of effrontery that I reared her. The devil must have given her the itch, if I may be forgiven the expression. I am truly grieved, and I find myself wondering why the fates have conspired to bring such news to me at this age. There is no way, I fear, to convey to you the shame and remorse I feel.*

*The circumstances being as you have described them, you can hardly be expected, in your indignation, to take kindly to interference. There are nevertheless certain matters which must be discussed, and I shall have to take the liberty of asking whether you and Misako could in the near future visit me. I shall discuss the problem with her in a friendly manner and attempt to make her see her folly, and if she appears not to be in a penitent mood I shall punish her as seems proper. I must ask you most humbly to forgive her should she wish to reform.*

*I was fortunate enough to find a puppet, and would have written you of it immediately but for a stiffness in the shoulder, which stiffness I was still nursing when this bewildering news arrived. An old man may perhaps be forgiven for complaining that his pilgrimage seems to have won him no grace, that he seems to have earned for himself only the wrath of the Buddha.*

*I shall be waiting for you whenever it is possible for you to come; even tomorrow would not be too soon. And please—I must be emphatic—do nothing extreme until we have had our talk.*

"This will never do." Kaname handed the letter to Misako. " 'I am truly grieved, and I find myself wondering why the fates have conspired to bring such tidings to me.' "

"What in the world did you say to him?"

"I tried to put it as simply as I could without leaving out the important part. I did everything I could to show him that neither of us was any more wrong than the other. I said that I was responsible too, and that I wanted a divorce as much as you did."

"I knew what sort of answer you would get, though."

But to Kaname it was a surprise. Misako had argued

124

that the news must be broken face to face, that if one tried to explain through a letter, mistakes were sure to arise. Kaname had not been able to answer the argument very successfully, but there were reasons why he had felt he must first send off a warning, and after a few days go for a conference. He wanted to lessen the shock as much as he could, and he knew that, after those pleasant days on Awaji when he had not so much as hinted that anything was amiss, he would not be able to bring the matter up without having sent off a preliminary explanation. Then too, as the letter showed clearly enough, the old man would think he had come to see the puppet. To interrupt the proud story of the new acquisition with unpleasant news would be too cruel. Surely one could have expected the old man to be a little more understanding, in view of his own hardly puritanical past. He liked to let it be known that he was an uncompromising gentleman of the old school. That, however, was an affectation, a hobby of sorts, common enough with men his age, and when it came to practical and immediate matters he ought really to be a little more up with the times. Not only had he refused to take Kaname's letter in the spirit in which it was intended, but his own letter was full of phrases that showed a complete misreading of even its literal sense. "You can hardly be expected, in your indignation," and "There is no way, I fear, to convey to you the shame and remorse I feel." Had he deigned to read only what Kaname had written, he would surely not have felt called upon to mention his "shame." Kaname had taken great pains to phrase his letter in terms that could arouse neither accusations nor apologies. But perhaps the old man's letter, full as it was of formal rhetorical flights, was to be taken as no more than a gesture demanded by his standards of good form.

"I think you can discount a lot of this. When you write an old-fashioned letter you pretty well have to say old-fashioned things. Probably he did it just for the fun of being old-fashioned, and I doubt if he's really as upset as he pretends to be. Only annoyed to have something like this cut him off when he wants to talk about his puppet."

Misako was a little pale, but she tried to make it

125

appear that the matter disturbed her not in the least, that she was quite above it. Her face was expressionless.

"What are you going to do?" Kaname asked.

"What am I going to do?"

"Are you going to Kyoto with me?"

"I couldn't bear to." It was clear from the way she threw out the words that she really couldn't. "Why don't you go by yourself and have it out with him?"

"You saw what he said. It would be better if you went along. It shouldn't be as hard as you think."

"I can't stand the idea of being lectured to in front of that O-hisa. I'll go after you have everything settled."

They were, for once, looking straight into each other's eyes, but Kaname found Misako's manner a little embarrassing. To hide her self-consciousness she flung her words at him with a certain harshness, blowing smoke rings from a gold-tipped cigarette all the while. Though she was probably not aware of it, her speech and her facial expressions were changing. Perhaps it was Aso's influence. Perhaps she was taking over his mannerisms. It was at times like this that Kaname was most painfully aware of how far from him his wife had gone. She was no longer a part of his house. In her choice of words, the tone of her speech, there was something that might still be said to carry his family name, but he could see it disappearing. He had not been prepared for the pain that came with the realization, and he sensed something of the pain that the final scene, pressing so close, must bring. It occurred to him, however, that his wife had in a way already disappeared. The Misako he saw here—was she not an entirely new person? She had —who knows when?—slipped free of her past and the destiny it had carried with it. Kaname found that sad, but the sadness seemed rather different from regret. And so, perhaps, the final crisis that he so dreaded had already passed. . . .

"What was in Takanatsu's letter?" he asked.

"He has business in Osaka again before long, but he doesn't want to see us until everything is decided. He says he'll probably go back to China without stopping by here."

"And that's all?"

"Well—" Misako was sitting on the veranda. With

one hand she rubbed her foot, and in the other she held a cigarette, flicking the ashes into the garden. The azaleas were in full bloom. "He did mention something. He said he would leave it to me whether I wanted to tell you or not."

"Oh?"

"He said he went ahead without asking us and told Hiroshi everything."

"Takanatsu did?"

"Yes."

"When?"

"When they were in Tokyo together. During spring vacation."

"Why the devil did he do that?"

Even now, when he had gone so far as to tell the old man in Kyoto, Kaname had said not a word to Hiroshi. So the child knew everything, and had contrived to keep them from suspecting. It was moving and yet a little repelling.

"He said he didn't intend to, but it all started one night after they had gone to bed. He heard Hiroshi crying and wanted to know what was the matter."

"Then?"

"It was in a letter, after all, and he couldn't write everything. He told Hiroshi we might separate and I might go to live with Aso. Hiroshi wanted to know what would happen to him then, and Takanatsu said that he had nothing to worry about, that he could go on seeing me as though he had two houses, and that some day he would understand why it had happened. That was the sum of it."

"Was Hiroshi satisfied?"

"He didn't say anything. He cried himself to sleep. The next day Takanatsu watched to see how he had come through. They went to the Mitsukoshi, and Hiroshi asked for everything in the store, exactly as though nothing had happened. Takanatsu said he was sure the worst was over—he hadn't known how soon children forget."

"But it's not the same as if I had told him myself."

"Oh yes—he said too that he didn't think we needed to tell Hiroshi anything more if it bothered us to. He said he was sorry he had gone ahead without asking us, but he thought he had taken care of at least that much for us."

"It won't do. I may not be exactly decisive, but I have to have it a bit more definite than that."

Kaname had hoped to postpone telling Hiroshi to the very last moment of the very last scene, but he could hardly tell Misako his reason. He still felt that the near future could bring a sudden and complete change, that he really could not know yet what the final outcome would be. Misako was determined, of course, and yet her very hardness was somehow brittle and fragile, and under the surface she seemed consumed by the strongest doubts. It would take very little, Kaname thought, to make her collapse in tears. Both of them dreaded such a crisis and both of them were constantly on guard to avoid it, but even now as they talked to each other it seemed as though the workings of an instant could cancel out the distance they had come and put them back again at the beginning. He did not for a moment think that Misako would follow the old man's advice. Still, if she did, he himself would have no alternative but to follow along—somewhere in the depths of his consciousness that feeling persisted. Neither resigned nor hopeful, he was a little awed by it.

"If you'll excuse me, then—" The prospect of further discussion apparently too much for her, Misako glanced at the clock as though to signal that the usual hour for her to go out had come, and got up with a rather harried look to change her clothes.

"I've been putting it off, but do you think I ought to see Aso again some time myself?" Kaname asked.

"You really should. Before you go to Kyoto or after?"

"Which would be best?"

" 'Even tomorrow would not be too soon.' Maybe you'd better go to Kyoto first. It would be a nuisance if Father were to come here, and besides, once everything is settled, Aso wants us to meet his mother."

"What did you do with Takanatsu's letter?" he called into the hall after her. No more than an attractive and appealing woman in a most womanly rush to be off to her lover, she seemed to him.

"I left it somewhere to show you, I've forgotten where.

128

Won't it do as well if I look when I get back? I've told you fairly well what he said, anyway."

"It really doesn't matter."

After Misako had left, Kaname went out to feed the dogs, a biscuit to one and a biscuit to the other in turns. He helped Jiiya brush them, then went into the small breakfast room and absently lay down.

"O-sayo! . . . Someone!"

He would have liked some tea, but the maids were evidently shut in their rooms and no one answered. Hiroshi was not yet back from school. Kaname felt lonely and abandoned in the quiet house. Ought he perhaps to go to see Louise again? Always at times like this the urge came upon him, but today for some reason he pitied himself more than usual. Always he found himself reconsidering that vow to stay away from her, pointing out to himself the foolishness of being held to it—what if she was only a prostitute?—deciding that he would see her again; but today in addition he found the house unbearable. The sliding doors, the alcove decorations, the trees outside, were all in place and unchanged, and yet the whole seemed stark and gaping. The previous owner had built the house and lived in it only a year or two, and Kaname had bought it when they moved to Osaka. This room had been added on afterwards. Its fine-grained fir and cedar pillars had, almost untended, taken on a soft glow over the years, and presently they would have an overlay of age that would please even the old man in Kyoto. Lying on the matted floor, Kaname looked with new interest at the mellowed woodwork, at the stand in the alcove and the trailing branch of bright yellow flowers, at the polished wood in the hall reflecting the light from outside like water. For all the excitement of her love affair, Misako still changed the decorations in the Japanese rooms now and then, the hangings and the flowers, to harmonize with the changing of the seasons. No doubt she did it from inertia and habit. Still, when Kaname thought of the day when the flowers would disappear, he knew that even this lifeless marriage, like the sheen of woodwork seen and remembered morning and evening and morning again, was something so near and so familiar that it would continue to pull at him even after it was gone.

129

"O-sayo, bring me a towel," he called from the hall. Slipping off his serge summer kimono, he wiped the sweat from his back, then changed to the suit Misako had laid out. The old man's letter lay on the floor with the discarded kimono. He was about to put it into his coat pocket when he thought of Louise's coy habit ("Is this from a geisha?" she would say) of going through his pockets for letters. As he started to push it out of sight under the lining of the dresser drawer, his hand brushed against something. Misako had hidden Takanatsu's letter in the same drawer.

"I wonder if I ought to read it." He hesitated before he took it from the envelope. She had hidden it carefully and could hardly have forgotten where. He could see now how little she had wanted to show it to him—indeed, her harried manner had said as much. But she was not given to hiding things from him. The contents must be particularly unpleasant, he thought. It would not be kind to read it. Still—

DEAR MISAKO:

*Thank you for your letter. I had thought that by now everything would be decided, but the other day I got a postcard from Awaji and saw that nothing had been. Your letter therefore did not surprise me.*

Kaname went up to the second floor of the foreign wing to finish the letter at his ease.

*If your decision is really final, would it not be wise to carry it through as quickly as you can? There seems to be no other way open to you, as a matter of fact, now that you have come this far. Kaname humors himself too much and so do you, and this is the result, I cannot help thinking. I do not mind having you come weeping to me, but why not go weeping to him instead? ("Weeping" is perhaps unfair. I suppose you do not mean to sound quite so tearful.) You are unable to, of course—that I understand, and I can think of nothing sadder. But if you feel so much reserve, then surely you cannot stay married to him. "He gave me too much freedom," you say, or "I wish I had never met Aso." If you could say*

130

only a fraction of that directly to Kaname—if there were only that much frankness between you two as husband and wife—but I shall say no more. I begin to sound peevish. I shall of course not mention your letter to Kaname. It would serve no purpose, only make things worse. I must seem heartless to you, I know, though in fact I think of my own experience with Yoshiko and am more moved than I can tell you. It is only that I must not let myself get emotional. I must keep to the central problem, that of your misfortune in having arrived at a point where there is no course open to you but to leave Kaname. Forget about the past, start over with a new and happy home, I beseech you, and see that you do not make the same mistake again. Kaname too will be happier, I feel sure. You must not think I am angry. I do not have a very subtle mind, however, and I have become convinced that it is hardly my place to plunge into the middle of this complicated relationship of yours, that it would be much wiser for me to stay away until you have made your own decision. I have delayed my sailing in the hope that you might make it soon, but it seems now that I shall have to take care of my business in Osaka and leave again without seeing you. I am sure you will understand.

There is something I have kept from you. I talked to Hiroshi when we were in Tokyo together. He took it very well, I thought. Have you noticed any change in him? I get letters now and then, though with never a mention of that evening. He is a bright lad—but do not think I am trying to beguile you into overlooking what I have done. If I have meddled more than I should, I apologize. Yet you will admit, I am sure, that it has been easier for me to tell him than it would have been for you. . . . Presumptuous though it may seem, I should like you to know that I want to do what little I can, as a relative and as the friend who knows them best, to help both Kaname and Hiroshi. I believe that both of them can stand a shock. The way through life is not always smooth, and it is good for a boy to have his troubles. Indeed, Kaname himself has had all too few. A really serious blow might teach him to pamper himself a little less.

131

*Good-by for now. I shall look forward to seeing you when you are married again.*

May 27

It was for Takanatsu an unusually long letter. Kaname's eyes were filled with tears when he finished reading. Perhaps the empty house had weakened his defenses.

## CHAPTER FOURTEEN

CALL them part of the family if you would, they were still guests. O-hisa had arranged the star lilies in the alcove that morning and retouched them to the proper angles several times during the day. At a little after four she caught a glimpse through the summer blind of a parasol coming in under the greenery at the gate. She stepped out into the garden.

"They're here?" the old man asked as he heard her wooden clogs behind him. He had gone out after his nap to clean caterpillar nests from the shrubbery.

"They're here."

"Misako too?"

"I believe so."

"Fine, fine. You get tea ready." He followed the steppingstones around the house and out the wicker garden gate. "Come in, come in," he called cheerfully. "It must have been a warm trip."

"It was warm," Kaname agreed. "We should have come this morning, but somehow it was noon before we got ourselves started."

"You really should have. The minute you think the weather is good, you find it's as sultry as the middle of August. But please come in."

Kaname and Misako followed him into the house. The bamboo summer mats, reflecting the green of the June foliage up from the floor, were cool against their stockinged feet. There was a faint smell of incense—a

132

grass seed, they would have guessed—through the house.

"But I forgot. You'll want to cool yourselves off a bit first. O-hisa, bring some towels." The old man, looking covertly for clues to their intentions, noticed that Kaname's face was wet with perspiration and mirrored the green from outside. The garden was shaded to a faint dusk by the trees, and the room was darker still. They had taken seats where the breeze passed, out near the veranda.

"Wouldn't hot towels really be better?" asked O-hisa.

"I suppose so. And you might take off your coat, Kaname."

"Thank you. . . . Your mosquitoes seem to be out even in the daytime."

"Indeed they are. Honjo has nothing on us—they say it's New Year before the mosquitoes are gone from Honjo, you know. Ours here are big dry-land ones, worse than any they have in Honjo. We could use ordinary mosquito-repellent, I suppose, but chrysanthemums aren't quite so unpleasant. We keep them burning here in a baking-dish."

As Kaname had expected, the old man showed none of the dismay his letter had suggested. He was calm and amiable as ever, quite ignoring Misako, who sat glumly outside the conversation. O-hisa too was her usual tranquil self, even though she had no doubt been told of Kaname's letter. She brought in tea and towels, almost noiselessly, and disappeared. There was no trace of her through all the rooms that were visible, open for the summer, beyond light reed blinds.

"You can stay tonight, can't you?" the old man asked.

"We could, yes. . . . We came without deciding definitely, though." Kaname glanced for the first time at his wife.

"I'm going back," she said almost defiantly. "Can't you have your talk and be finished early?"

"Misako, we'd like to be alone for a few minutes." The quiet of the room was broken by a faint puff as the old man blew the ashes from his pipe. Misako left the room and went upstairs—O-hisa, she was afraid, might still be somewhere below—while he was refilling it and lighting it from a charcoal ember.

"We have a problem, haven't we?"

133

"I'm sorry we've had to upset you so. We haven't said anything before because we've thought perhaps we might find a way out without coming to this."

"And now you can't?"

"I'm afraid we can't. I tried to cover everything in my letter. . . . There must be parts of it you will want explained, though."

"No, no—I understand in a general way. But, Kaname, if you want my opinion in a word, I say you're in the wrong."

Startled at the directness, Kaname opened his mouth to answer. The old man cut him off and continued:

"I suppose that is a little too strong. But don't you think you put too much faith in what you call being reasonable? The times are what they are, and I can't keep you from treating your wife as if she were another man of the world, I suppose. You shouldn't be surprised, though, if you find it doesn't work as you think it ought to. But let me come to the point and forget the preliminaries. You had Misako choose another husband on a trial basis because you didn't have the qualifications yourself, you say. That's not very realistic. You talk about being modern, but there are some things you simply can't do in that free, open way of yours."

"I can't argue with you if that's the tone you're going to take."

"Wait, Kaname. You may think I'm being sarcastic, but I'm saying what I feel very strongly. In the old days there were any number of couples like you and Misako. My wife and I were that way ourselves, as a matter of fact. . . . None of your one year or two years—sometimes for five years at a stretch I never went near her. But she just assumed that was the way things were, and there was no problem. The world has come to be a much more complicated place, when you think about it. . . . But if you send a woman away, even for a trial, and she discovers halfway through that she's made a mistake, then she's in the predicament of not being able to come back, no matter how much she may want to. Talk of 'free choice' all you like, there's no free choice whatsoever in the matter. I don't know about your woman of the future, but Misako's education has been half old and half new, and all this modernness of hers is a pretty thin veneer."

"Mine is thin too. In a way we're hurrying the divorce along because we both know it. And in the final analysis I do think we're doing the right thing."

"I'll never tell her you said so, Kaname, but leaving the problem of Misako to me, would it be possible for you yourself to reconsider? I won't argue with you, maybe because old people want peace at any price. If the two of you aren't suited for each other, though, if you think you're not compatible, don't worry too much about it. Time will pass and you'll find that you are very much suited for each other after all. O-hisa's far younger than I, and we aren't what you could call well matched, but when two people live together, an affection does develop, and somehow they get by while they're waiting for it to. Can't you say after all that that's what a marriage is? But of course Misako's been unfaithful, and I can't blame you if you tell me I'm talking nonsense."

"Please—that has nothing to do with it. She had my permission, and it's not fair to call her unfaithful."

"But unfaithfulness is unfaithfulness. I only wish you'd told me before it came to that."

Silence seemed the only possible reply to the soft reproach. There was room for rebuttal, but the old man was not really so unreasonable as to have rejected the explanation Kaname had already made. There lay behind the words a father's sorrow that Kaname felt he had to respect.

"I could have done better in many ways, I suppose," he began finally. "I sometimes tell myself it would have been better if I had done this or that. But it's all past now, and the main thing is that Misako has definitely made up her mind."

It was getting darker outside. Shadows deepened in the corners of the room. The old man knelt, fanning at the smoke from the smoldering chrysanthemums. The lines of his knees, thin perhaps from the heat, were sharply marked under the fine stripes of his kimono. He seemed to be blinking rapidly, as though his eyes smarted. Possibly it was Kaname's fancy. Or possibly the smoke.

"You're right, of course. It was not clever of me to talk to you first. Anyway, you will let me have Misako for two or three hours?"

"I'm sure it will do you no good. As a matter of fact,

she dreaded having to talk to you—that's the real reason we're so late. We would have come sooner, but time went by while we argued. It really was something of a battle to get her to come even this late. Finally she agreed, but said that her mind was made up and that I'd have to do all the talking, and the listening if you had anything to say."

"But after all, Kaname, even if the divorce has to come, I'm not to be brushed aside quite as simply as that."

"So I kept telling her. Anyway, she's excited and upset and would rather not quarrel with you, and she wants me to act as her agent somehow and get your blessing —that I'm sure is how she feels. Shall we have her come in?"

"No, what I have in mind—I think O-hisa has something ready, but I could take Misako out to dinner. You won't object, will you?"

"I don't think it will be easy to persuade her."

"I know that. I'll see what I can do. If she says she won't go, then that's all there is to it, but maybe we can arrange so that there will be something left to flatter the whims of an old man." He clapped for O-hisa and gave her instructions while Kaname sat fidgeting. "Could you call the Hyōtei, please? Tell them there will be two of us, and we'd like a quiet room."

"Two of you are going out?"

"You've probably put all your art into dinner, and it seems wrong to clear out all your guests."

"But that's not fair to the one who has to stay. Wouldn't it be better for everyone to go?"

"What can you offer your guests?"

"Nothing decent."

"The salmon roe?"

"I thought I might deep-fry the salmon roe."

"And what else?"

"Baked trout—"

"And?"

"And a salad."

"Well, Kaname, the food to go with it doesn't sound very promising, but maybe you could stay and have a few drinks."

"Poor Kaname gets the booby prize."

"Really, now," Kaname protested, "the cook is better

than the cook at the Hyōtei. I'll have myself a feast."

"Would you lay my clothes out, then?" The old man started upstairs.

Kaname could not guess what the decisive arguments might have been, but they were perhaps not too different from the ones he had used himself on the way up from Osaka: "If you cross him, you may find your last chance gone for getting through this safely." In any case, fifteen minutes or so later Misako came darkly down the stairs. She retouched her face in the doorway and without a word went out ahead of her father.

"We'll see you later." The old man slipped his white-stockinged feet into his sandals. He had on a silk-gauze cap and looked ready for the role of a poet on the stage.

"Hurry back," said O-hisa.

"We may not be able to hurry exactly. . . . I've already spoken to Misako about it, Kaname. We'll expect you to stay the night."

"But we're making nuisances of ourselves. . . . Not that I wouldn't like to stay myself."

"Bring me an umbrella, O-hisa. It's got sultry. It will probably be raining again before long."

"Suppose you take a taxi," suggested O-hisa.

"Nothing of the sort. It's much too near. We can walk."

"Have a good time." O-hisa saw them to the gate, and a moment or so later followed Kaname back into the front room with a terry-cloth bath kimono over her arm. "And now how would you like a bath? It's ready whenever you say."

"You're being very kind. I wonder if I should, though. I'll never be able to pick myself up and go back to Osaka afterwards."

"But you're staying the night."

"I'm not at all sure that we are."

"Don't say that. Anyway, you're not going to have much of a dinner, and I want you at least to be hungry."

Kaname did not know when he had last been in this bath. A typical Kyoto bath, so small that one could hardly sit in it comfortably and so sharp to the touch with its heated metal sides that one accustomed to soaking at his leisure in the ample wooden Tokyo bathtub could never feel afterwards that he had had a bath at all. It was made still more inhospitable by the gloom. The one small

137

latticed window up near the ceiling admitted little enough light even during the brightest part of the day. Then, too, Kaname was used to a tiled bathroom at home, and he always found taking a bath here rather like being shut up in a dark cellar. The water, perfumed with cloves, suggested nothing so much as a cloudy, sediment-filled medicine bath. Misako held that the cloves were a trick to hide the dirty water, that there was no telling how many days it had gone unchanged, and she always managed to escape when she was urged to have a bath. The old man, however, was proud of his "clove bath." It was a particular treat he was able to offer his guests.

He had developed his private scatological philosophy, something like this: "A pure white bath or toilet is a piece of Western foolishness. It matters little, you may say, because no one is around to see, but a device that sets your own sewage out in front of your eyes is highly offensive to good taste. How much more proper to dispose of it modestly in as dark and out-of-the-way a corner as you can find." He advocated stuffing the urinal with fresh green cedar twigs, it being his eccentric view that "a well-tended toilet in the pure Japanese style should have a delicate odor all its own. That gives one an inexpressible feeling of elegance and refinement." The toilet aside, O-hisa complained privately about the dark bath. And it would serve quite as well, she said, to perfume it with a drop or two of the essence of cloves one can buy these days, but the old man would be satisfied only with the old way, the bag of clove heads stewing in the tub.

"He offers to wash my back sometimes, but it's so dark he can't tell front from back," O-hisa had once confessed. Kaname's eye fell on a bran bag, the old Japanese substitute for soap, hanging from a pillar.

"How is it?" O-hisa's voice came from outside, where she was putting wood in the water-heater.

"Splendid. But if it wouldn't be too much trouble, could you turn on the light, please?"

"I'm sorry. I did forget the light, didn't I?"

The light—no doubt that too had its reasons—was a tiny night bulb that seemed only to intensify the gloom. As Kaname stepped out of his kimono, he was assailed by mosquitoes all over his body. He hurriedly wiped away the sweat, not bothering to wash himself as thoroughly as he might, and began soaking with the cloves. The mosquitoes hummed round his face and neck. For all the darkness inside, there seemed still to be a soft evening light in the garden, and the maple leaves through the high latticed window glowed a clearer, fresher green, like a silken fabric, than they had in the full daylight. He felt as though he were far away at some secluded mountain resort. "You can hear cuckoos in my garden," the old man was fond of boasting, and Kaname strained his ears to pick up a cuckoo's call even now. All he could hear, however, was a frog in some distant paddy prophesying rain, and the steady humming of the mosquitoes. What would the old man and Misako be doing in their restaurant? The old man had been reticent in front of his son-in-law, but his manner had suggested that he might apply considerable pressure when he had his daughter alone. Kaname was a little uneasy at the thought; but it did not dispel the vague light-heartedness he had felt since he saw the two of them off.

He was taken with the odd fancy that this house, here where he was soaking in the bath, was his own house now that he had divorced Misako and begun a new life. Deep down he may have had unsuspected motives, it occurred to him, for seeking out the company of the old man these last few months. He had cherished a dream in secret, an extraordinary dream, and he had neither cautioned himself nor reproved himself for it. That may have been because O-hisa was to him less a specific person than a "type O-hisa." It would probably suit him as well if he had not this particular O-hisa, ministering to the old man here, but another who belonged to "type O-hisa." The O-hisa for whom his secret dream searched might not be O-hisa at all, but another, a more O-hisa-like O-hisa. And it might even be that this latter O-hisa was no more than a doll, perhaps even now quiet in the dusk of an inner chamber behind an arched stage doorway. A doll might do well enough, indeed.

"I feel much better," he said, as if he hoped the sound of his voice might drive off these strange fancies. The terry cloth was cool against his skin.

"You must have been uncomfortable in such a dirty bath."

"On the contrary, a clove bath is a good change now and then."

"But a bright bathroom like yours—it's not for me, I'm afraid."

"Why do you say that?"

"Everything so pure and white, everything so bright —to someone as good-looking as Misako I suppose it doesn't matter."

"Is she as good-looking as all that?" A note of derision, of hostility toward his absent wife, crept into Kaname's voice. He quickly emptied the first cup of saké O-hisa had poured for him. "But won't you have some yourself?"

"Thank you. Perhaps I shall."

"The salmon roe is excellent. . . . How are you coming with the music?"

"Oh, that—tedious, monotonous."

"You aren't practicing any more?"

"I go on with it. Misako sings the Tokyo way, I suppose."

"I suspect she graduated from that long ago and has gone on to jazz."

O-hisa drove a moth from the clear-lacquer table, the breeze from her fan cool through Kaname's light kimono. The clean smell of spring mushrooms rose faintly from the soup. It was pitch-dark now in the garden, and the croaking of the rain-frogs had risen to a clamor.

"I'd like to learn the Tokyo style myself."

"You'll be scolded for dangerous thoughts. And I'm afraid I'll have to join the scolding—you've no idea how much better the Osaka style is for you."

"I don't object to it so much. But the teacher is rather a problem."

"Let me see—you go to someone in Osaka, don't you?"

"That's right. But I was thinking more of the teacher here."

Kaname laughed.

"He's unbearable. Lecture, lecture, lecture."

"All old people are that way." Kaname laughed again.

"That reminds me. I noticed the bran bag. You still use it?"

"That's right. He uses soap himself, but he won't let me. He says women mustn't ruin their skin with soap."

"And the nightingale dung?"

"I go on with that too. But it hasn't made my skin a bit whiter."

Kaname was finishing off the meal with his second decanter of saké, and O-hisa had brought in a dish of loquats when the telephone rang. She ran to answer it, leaving a half-peeled loquat in an antique glass saucer.

"Yes . . . yes . . . I see. I'll tell him." Kaname could see her in the hall nodding into the telephone. In a minute or two she was back. "Misako will stay too, he says. They'll be home before long."

"Really? And she said she wouldn't. . . . It seems an awfully long time since I last spent the night here."

"It has been a long time."

More than that, though, it seemed a long time since he and Misako had slept alone together. There had of course been those two or three nights—their first alone in he did not know how many years—when Hiroshi was in Tokyo with Takanatsu; but they had been able then to lie down side by side and go off to sleep as unconcernedly as two strangers at an inn, so deadened had their marital nerves become. He suspected that tonight, however, the old man hoped for great changes to come from throwing them together. This benevolent scheming was a little disconcerting, but not enough so that Kaname felt pressed to try for an escape. He was sure that the time had passed when one night could make a difference.

"Hasn't it grown heavy?" said Kaname. "Not a breath of air." He looked out to the veranda. The incense, on the point of going out, sent a column of smoke straight and unwavering into the air. The breeze in the garden had died, and with it the breeze from O-hisa's fan, motionless in her lap and as though forgotten.

"It's clouding over. I wonder if it will rain."

"It might well. I almost hope it will."

Above the motionless leaves a star here and there broke through the clouds. For a moment he thought he could hear, as with a sixth sense, Misako's voice fighting back the old man; and he knew that almost unconsciously he had come to a point where he could support his wife's decision with an even stronger one of his own.

"What time do you suppose it is?"

"Eight thirty, possibly."

"Only eight thirty. Isn't it quiet, though?"

"It's still early, but you may want to go to bed. They should be back before long."

"I suppose it seemed from what he said over the telephone that the conversation was not going very well?" Kaname was secretly more interested in having O-hisa's views than the old man's.

"Shall I bring you something to read?"

"Thank you. What sort of things do you read?"

"He brings home old wood-block books and tells me I should read them. But I can't get interested in the dusty old things."

"You'd rather read a woman's magazine?"

"He says if I have time for that sort of trash I should be practicing my calligraphy."

"What copybook does he have you on?"

"There are a couple. *O-ie* method."

"Well, let me look at one of your dusty books."

"How about a travel guide?"

"That should do, I suppose."

"Let's go out to the cottage, then. I have everything ready."

O-hisa led the way along a covered passage to the garden cottage. As she slid back the paper-paneled door to the rear of the tearoom, Kaname caught the rustling of a mosquito net in the darkness beyond. A cool breath of air came through the open door.

"The wind seems to have come up again."

"And all of a sudden it's a little chilly," Kaname answered. "We'll have a shower before long."

The mosquito net rustled again, this time not from the wind. O-hisa felt her way inside and, groping for the lamp at Kaname's pillow, turned the switch.

"Shall I get you a larger bulb?"

"This will do nicely. The print's always big in old books."

"Suppose I leave the shutters open. You won't want it too hot."

"I wish you would. I can close them later."

142

Kaname crawled under the net himself when O-hisa had gone. The room was not a large one, and the linen mosquito netting cut it off smaller yet, so that the two mattresses were almost touching. It was a novel arrangement for Kaname and Misako. At home these summer nights they hung up as large a mosquito net as possible and slept, one at each end, with Hiroshi between them. Kaname rolled over on his stomach, a little bored, and lighted a cigarette. He tried to make out the picture in the alcove beyond the light-green netting. Something in modest, neutral colors, a landscape it seemed to be, wider than it was high. With the light inside the net, however, the rest of the room lay in deep shadow, and he could make out neither the details nor the artist's signature. Below it in a bowl was what he took to be a blue and white porcelain burner. There was a faint smell of incense through the room—he noticed it for the first time. Plum blossom, he judged. For an instant he thought he saw O-hisa's face, faint and white, in a shadowy corner beside the bed. He started up, but quickly caught himself. It was the puppet the old man had brought back from Awaji, a lady puppet in a modest dotted kimono.

A gust of wind came through the open window and the shower began. Kaname could hear large drops falling against the leaves. He raised himself on an elbow and stared out into the wooded depths of the garden. A small green frog, a refugee from the rain, clung halfway up the fluttering side of the net, its belly reflecting the light from the bed lamp.

"It's finally begun."

The door slid open, and this time, half a dozen old-style Japanese books in arm, it was no puppet that sat faintly white in the shadows beyond the netting.

(Please turn page)

You'll also want to read . . .

## SNOW COUNTRY
### by Yasunari Kawabata

Somewhere in the depths of your mind you will find you have lived in the cold, snowy air, seen the landscape, stopped over in the inns, spent the night with the geishas, and even longed for the spring that seems so far away from . . .

## SNOW COUNTRY

The passionate story of a geisha's affair in an exotic pleasure resort.

"A vignette of Oriental decadence, beautifully presented . . . a work of art."
                    —San Francisco Chronicle

This book available at your local newsstand, or send 35¢ plus 10¢ per copy for mailing costs to Berkley Publishing Corp., 101 Fifth Avenue, New York 3, New York.